W9-BDQ-294

What the critics are saying:

"Reader favorites Cheyenne McCray and Annie Windsor collaborate on this yummy vampire tale for a double dose of sexy adventure. VAMPIRE DREAMS is an intriguing alternate reality story that will thrill you, excite you, touch you, and sate you." - *Cynthia, A Romance Review*

"I applaud Cheyenne McCray and Annie Windsor on their successful collaboration with VAMPIRE DREAMS. The writing is flawless, and the story flows without a hitch." - *Sinclair Reid, Romance Reviews Today*

"Ms. McCray and Ms. Windsor make a dynamic writing duo... VAMPIRE DREAMS starts hot and heavy and does not let up... This story is extremely fast paced and definitely worth journey!" - *Sara Sawyer, The Romance Studio*

"The sex is intense, frequent and totally blows the mind, so keep the ice handy. The plot will have you on the edge of your seat and you won't put it down until it's done. The awesome duo of Cheyenne McCray and Annie Windsor is an incredible combination and I can only hope that these two great authors decide to do another book in the future." - *Angel Brewer, Just Erotic Romance Reviews*

"A tale of long lost love reclaimed, human betrayal avenged and familial ties reformed, VAMPIRE DREAMS provides great action, both on the streets and in between the sheets." - *Brenda Edde, Romance Junkies*

Discover for yourself why readers can't get enough of the multiple award-winning publisher Ellora's Cave. Whether you prefer e-books or paperbacks, be sure to visit EC on the web at www.ellorascave.com for an erotic reading experience that will leave you breathless.

WWW.ELLORASCAVE.COM

VAMPIRE DREAMS
An Ellora's Cave Publication, September 2004

Ellora's Cave Publishing, Inc.
PO Box 787
Hudson, OH 44236-0787

ISBN #1-4199-5028-2

ISBN MS Reader (LIT) ISBN # 1-84360-855-3
Other available formats (no ISBNs are assigned):
Adobe (PDF), Rocketbook (RB), Mobipocket (PRC) & HTML

VAMPIRE DREAMS © 2004 CHEYENNE MCCRAY & ANNIE
WINDSOR

ALL RIGHTS RESERVED. This book may not be reproduced in
whole or in part without permission.

This book is a work of fiction and any resemblance to persons,
living or dead, or places, events or locales is purely coincidental.
They are productions of the authors' imagination and used
fictitiously.

Edited by *Heather Osborn*
Cover art by *Syneca*

VAMPIRE DREAMS

Cheyenne McCray & Annie Windsor

To Debbie and Susan

Without whom Vampire Dreams wouldn't have been possible

Acknowledgment

*Thank you, Maryam, Patti, and Claudia
You're the best!*

Prologue
Deep of the Night

Come with me, the bell is already ringing, your eyes will be my single shelter…

Words from *The Soldadera Corrido* rolled through her mind, bold like so many Mexican folk songs.

Why this tune about death and battle?

Why now?

Her confusion rose, and then…

He came to her as he always did.

Outside the open patio doors, moonlight played across the desert. The music in her mind stopped abruptly. She caught a glimpse of his shadowed jaw, high cheekbones, and the flash of dark eyes.

She stood beside her bed, her body humming, aware of every movement he made as he silently slipped through the patio doors and glided over the tiled floor. Sheer curtains billowed from either side of the doors, as if wanting to caress him as much as she did.

The fluttering sensation in her belly grew the closer he came, and her heart pounded in anticipation. He wore leather pants and boots, but left his chest bare. Well-cut muscles flexed as he moved. His stride was slow, purposeful, and his gaze never wavered from hers. She wanted to run to him, to throw her arms around him and beg him for his kisses.

But she was afraid he would vanish…again.

Come, come with me…

When he finally reached her, he paused for a moment and took her in with a long, hungry gaze. He smelled of night wind and the elemental scent of everything strong and male. Even though he stood but a breath away, as always, she couldn't quite make out his features. His long, dark hair stirred about his shoulders when a breeze swirled in through the patio doors, and she caught the flash of white teeth as he gave her a slow, sensual smile.

Beneath her silken bathrobe she trembled. With every breath her nipples rasped against the white silk. The ache between her thighs magnified and she felt herself grow damp with the incredible desires this man stirred.

"*Querida*," he murmured in his deep, vibrant voice as he reached out to cup her cheek.

"You came." She leaned into his touch, needing to feel as much of him as he was willing to give her. His palm felt warm against her skin and she sighed. Her eyelids fluttered and almost shut, but she didn't want to lose one moment of this encounter, or one second of seeing him.

"I missed you, my love." He brushed his lips over her forehead, and this time she couldn't help herself. She leaned into him, needing to savor his body against hers. He felt solid and so very real.

Tentatively, she scaled his bare chest with her fingertips until she touched the dark hair brushing his broad shoulders. His skin felt cool, and yet fire traveled the length of their joined flesh.

His hand slid from her face, down the curve of her neck. With a whisper-soft brush of his fingers, he slipped aside her robe, baring her shoulder.

She stood, heart thundering, knowing this was it, the moment of complete vulnerability. He could use her, or kill her, or any number of horrors in between—but he wouldn't. He never had.

As her body ached and throbbed, he lowered his head and pressed his mouth to her neck. She had a sensation of singing in her blood, of the veins in her neck straining to open and pour out her life for him, only him, always him. Her mind reeled as she felt the sweet, rough scrape of his teeth when he nipped at her. She shivered and clung to him as his mouth continued from her neck to her shoulder, kissing, sampling, nibbling. He swirled his tongue along her skin. She clasped her hands more firmly around his neck and completely melted against his solid, tensed body. His cock grew harder and harder against her belly, and she ached to feel him deep inside her. To feel his power, his possession, and the heat they shared.

Come, come with me…

With a groan he stepped away, forcing her to release him. She whimpered, but he didn't leave as she had feared he would. Instead he moved his hands to the tie of her robe, unraveling it and letting it flutter away. Her gaze followed the strip of silk to the floor and then returned to those darker-than-dark eyes. They flamed, then smoldered with passion so intense she could *feel* the predator in his soul, yearning to break free and consume her.

Maybe this time he would stay. Please, let him stay, let him make her feel this way day after day, night after night.

She didn't dare to breathe as he pulled open her robe. He audibly sucked in his breath as moonlight spilled across her naked breasts and mound.

"You are beautiful, *querida*." He pushed her robe from her other shoulder, letting the soft material slide down her arms until it landed in a swirl of silk at her feet.

"Touch me," she whispered. "Please."

He weakened her knees with that carnal smile. "I will do so much more than touch you."

She tensed as he raised his hands and cupped her breasts, and then moaned at the feel of him tweaking and rolling her nipples between his thumbs and forefingers. So sure of himself, this man. And the touch was familiar and intimate, forbidden and maddening all at once. He had her completely at his mercy, with no more than a few sizzling pinches. Bolts of heat traveled the length of her body each time he pressed her nipples, eased back, then pressed again. When he lowered his head and flicked his tongue across one taut bud, she cried out from the incredible pleasure. He moved to her other breast and suckled at the nipple and she nearly wept, the sensation was so exquisite. She did weep when he stopped.

In an effortless movement, he scooped her up in his strong arms and gently laid her on the bed. Her breasts ached where he had touched the tips. She wanted his hands, his mouth back on her, exploring, kissing, biting. But he only watched her with that intense gaze, his face still shadowed as if a sort of darkness shrouded him.

She shivered beneath the force of his stare.

What did he want from her?

Nothing? Everything?

Come, come with me...

With the lightest of touches, he skimmed his knuckles between her breasts, down the line of her belly to the curls of her mound. He gently teased the curls, then slid one finger deep into her wet folds.

She could do nothing but moan and arch into his touch, wanting more, needing more. But he brought his fingers from between her thighs and raised his hand to his mouth. Slowly, he slipped his finger between his lips and tasted her.

He closed his eyes for the briefest of moments and when he withdrew his finger he gave a soft groan.

Before she could catch her breath, before she even saw him move, he was on the bed, between her legs, hands braced to either side of her head. She gasped at the feel of his leather-clad hips between her thighs and the hard length of his cock pressing against her mound.

Without thought, she reached for the waistband of his pants and unfastened them. He merely watched her as she released his cock. She couldn't see from her vantage point, but she could feel it, oh, yes. Long, thick, and hot. She couldn't wait to have him inside her.

"Yes, *querida*," he murmured as she guided him to the opening of her wet channel. "We will be together."

The bell is already ringing…

Ecstasy built like a rogue wave, rushing from her head to her breasts to her belly, then down, down, to the point where they were about to join. Her body fell captive to the sensations. She needed this more than breath, more than safety, more than anything she had ever experienced or possessed.

The head of his cock began to push into her core. Finally. Ah, sweet heavens, finally. Yes. Yes!

And then he dissolved and vanished, like mist on the wind, leaving her empty, aching, and so, so coldly alone.

"No!" Hannah Cordova bolted upright in bed, grasping at the shreds of her erotic dream. "Not again. Damn." She groaned and covered her face with her hands.

This dream had been more real than any of the previous ones, and she'd been so close. *So* close! Her body throbbed and burned, crying out for his touch, screaming with frustrated desire.

She threw herself back on her pillow and stared up at the ceiling. Shadows chased one another across the white surface. A breeze blew across her skin and she glanced to see her patio doors open and the sheer curtains billowing like they had in the dream.

Your eyes will be my single shelter…

"I wish," she muttered, trying to shut off the ever-present music in her head. With a resigned sigh, Hannah reached into her nightstand drawer for her vibrator. It wasn't much, but it would ease the fire between her legs—and she might be able to breathe again.

At least she had her fantasies, her lover from the world of sleep and wishes.

As the hard, humming plastic pushed her toward a climax nowhere near as satisfying as the one she had almost dreamed, she battled back tears.

Why did she have to dream about perfection?
And why couldn't perfection be real?

Chapter One
Evening

Humming *De Colores*, the version she'd played at her last concert, Hannah pressed her foot on the gas pedal, urging the rental car along the desert highway. Strands of black hair escaped the chic knot at the base of her neck and teased her high cheekbones.

"That's it. That's it." She coaxed her creativity, letting the traditional song slide into a haunting melody she'd been working on during the trip. She'd flown into La Paz, Mexico, from Los Angeles, and then rented the car and driven south along the winding Mexican highways.

She needed some time for herself. Alone. Away from the limelight.

Away from Timothy Mix. Bastard. Betrayer. She'd been so stupid to go out with him—with any man! And how idiotic was it to tell him a few tender secrets? She'd thought he was real enough, human enough, man enough for a measure of confidence, but he'd splashed her private thoughts through every gossip rag in the world. Tears stung Hannah's eyes. She clenched the steering wheel so tight her knuckles ached, and the song died on her lips. International singing sensation, small-town girl turned star—and woman alone, unlikely to ever find the companionship she craved. The love she sang about so often in her songs—both the traditional folk music and more modern tunes—what a myth.

Only the yellow beams of the car's headlights cut through the darkness, and cacti stood like dark sentinels along the road. She had the windows open, night air blowing across her skin, alleviating some of the stress she'd stored during the week. It was almost summer, almost the change of seasons. Any other year, the scent of new life and all its potential would have thrilled Hannah. This season, however, she was still distracted and frustrated from spring's endless events.

Reaching back with one hand, she pulled the pin out of her hair and tossed it aside, letting the long mass ride free on the wind. It felt better to literally let her hair down, to relax and be just Hannah for a while. Not Hannah Cordova, recording artist rapidly losing control of her own life. Not Hannah the fool, whose heart had been bared to the world and broken while everyone stared and laughed.

If I want to be just Hannah, then why am I driving to Cabo San Lucas to meet Britt?

Hannah sighed.

Because she needed some time away with her best girlfriend. Britt was one of the few people who deserved her trust, and one of the few people who could help Hannah face what Timothy had done. Still, a trendy Mexican hotspot was the last place she should be going. What if the tabloid reporters were there, heaven forbid? Timothy had not only hurt her, but her family, too. How could she ever feel safe again—anywhere?

Hannah wished she could go back in time. Back to being the girl from Tucson with the good voice. Horrid, scathing tabloid gossip, two-faced and black-hearted men, vicious reporters who would sell their souls to Satan for a buck—those things would be problems for other people. Maybe people who could handle such treachery better than she could.

Miles of Highway 19 scrolled by, and the car purred as Hannah headed deeper into Baja California. She was far enough into the Mexican desert, away from the city glare, that stars glittered overhead like millions of tiny stage lights in the sky. It was early evening, the half moon just beginning to climb the night sky. Mixing with the smell of the ocean, a warm scent rose through the air, sweet and tangy, yet unlike anything she'd ever smelled before.

She usually enjoyed driving for hours, enjoyed being alone. Los Angeles was home now, but she'd grown up in the Arizona desert and she had to admit she missed it. Missed living a life in obscurity, a life where she had no one to answer to but herself. Well, that and her older sister Nicki, and her jerk of a boss at the local bank.

And her mom. She really missed her mother—how she used to be. Before all the confusion and babbling and accidental fire-setting. The problems started a few years back, right around the time Hannah took her folk-singing on the road and began to pursue her career in earnest. Nicki went with her, of course, but every time they came home, their mother seemed a little more distant. A little farther inside her own mind. They had tried clinics, specialists, medications—nothing stopped the problem. Every time they turned their back on her, she burned something else to ashes, and they couldn't even figure out where she was getting the matches. Finally, last spring, Hannah and Nicki had been forced to place their mother in a nursing facility for her own safety.

She could only pray that the tabloid assholes wouldn't find her. Hannah had purposefully stayed away from her family since her life story hit the newsstands just a week ago, not wanting to lead reporters to the ones she loved. Family bonds and privacy—hell, basic human decency—weren't sacred to those bastards, or to Timothy.

Hannah took deep, slow breaths, trying to banish the stress. She should at least hum or recite a poem, try to carry a tune out here, in the desert wind, where no one could hear. Singing was in Hannah's heart and soul, and she lived to perform. But sometimes she wished she could still sing in karaoke bars in Tucson. In the past year, during this wonderful and awful time when she'd been considered a rising star, she hadn't become used to being in the spotlight—to having so many people vying for her attention and her time. So much pressure, so many demands.

So many lies.

Hannah clenched her teeth. *I'm not going to cry, damn it! He's not worth it.*

Wind tossed her loose hair, combing through it like a lover might, a lover with long, skilled fingers. Hannah's thoughts became even more melancholy. If she had found an honest man instead of Timothy, a *real* man...

Like the one who constantly invaded her dreams — the good dreams, not the nightmares. The man who had started visiting her in her sleep years ago. Over time, chaste encounters with the dream man had become more and more erotic until she'd wake up in a cold sweat, aching and unfulfilled, just like this morning, before she'd left.

A vision filled her mind of the dream man's face, shadowed by darkness, as it always was. His body — what a wonder. The man could be one of Michelangelo's statues, with all that carved muscular perfection. So powerful. His hands felt so gentle and sensuous, yet he was strong and commanding. Even as she guided her car along the dark highway, Hannah could imagine how it would be to make love to him...a man who didn't care who she was, a man who wanted nothing more from her than her love. The man in her dreams would never lie to her, never take more than she was willing to give.

Something gave Hannah a bone-deep shiver. Abruptly, her dream-man vision ended, and she gripped the steering wheel with both hands. Had she been drifting out of her lane? Her head hurt, just a little pain, like a toothache.

In the distance she saw a wavering red light. Out in the middle of nowhere. Yet it was a welcoming light, and it seemed to draw her like a moth to flame.

Like men drawn to her money and fame. Like tabloids drawn to lies.

The ache behind her eyes faded, but her eyelids grew heavy as she motored toward the blood-red light. She slowed the vehicle down, squinting into the glare to make out the source of the red glow.

The light came from a large roadside sign.

Hotel Rojo.

Hannah blinked, fighting her exhaustion.

The sign's glow seemed to intensify.

She yawned. A tired weakness claimed her limbs, like she had worked out for far too long. Her traumatic week was definitely catching up with her.

Britt would be disappointed — but really, Hannah didn't think she could go any farther tonight. The pulsing red *Hotel Rojo* sign called her like a siren, whispering of soft beds and long, anonymous, uninterrupted sleep.

Another yawn brought tears to Hannah's eyes. Yes, she definitely had to stop and get a good night's sleep. She could call Britt at the hotel in Cabo and let her know she'd head out at first light tomorrow.

Hannah turned the car into the long paved driveway leading up to what appeared to be an exclusive resort. Palm trees lined the way, fronds swaying in the breeze, and the building gave her the impression of grandeur and luxury with its massive arches and rich wood detail. A gentle light came through hotel windows, making it seem even more welcoming.

She pulled into the circular driveway and parked directly in front of massive wooden doors carved with intricate Aztec designs. Ancient History had been one of her minors in college, before she was "discovered." She wasn't sure why, but she'd been completely fascinated by the history of the Aztecs who called themselves *Mexica*.

"*Me-shee-ca,*" Hannah murmured, intrigued.

She recognized Huitzilopochtli, the Aztec sun and war god, in a mosaic on the right hand door. The left door featured one of his mother, Coatlicue, the fearsome Earth goddess. Both mosaics had been created with minute tiles in brilliant hues of yellow, green, red, turquoise, and brown. On each side of the wooden doors burned torches, their flames flickering in the near darkness.

For a moment she sat in the rental car, mesmerized by the flames. Images flickered through her mind from her nightmares. Of being carried up carved stone steps to an altar bracketed by torches...

Hair at Hannah's nape prickled. Uneasy feelings broke like cold waves across her chest.

Leave now, a man said in her mind in a deep, penetrating tone that shocked her out of her trance. *Leave!* the male voice commanded again.

She shook her head, as if to rattle out the voice. What was wrong with her?

"Damn. Do I ever need a good night's sleep."

With her head high, she grabbed the keys and her purse and climbed out of the car. Her heels clicked on adobe paving as she walked toward the entrance. A woman stepped into the massive doorway, a soft glow of light coming from behind her. A doorman, clothed in traditional Aztec garb, held the door open.

Hannah gripped her keys and her purse tight in her hands as she focused on the woman. Countless braids and curls adorned her head, with emeralds and other precious gems woven throughout the black locks. Her regal bearing, bronzed skin, and colorful floor-length skirt gave her the appearance of Aztec nobility. She seemed ageless, with no wrinkles, not even fine lines at the corners of her eyes, yet those black eyes held the darkness of an ancient soul.

In the distance Hannah heard the ringing of a church bell.

The bell is already ringing, like in the folk song, in Soldadera Corrido...*only, I don't like this bell at all.*

The woman moved without moving, spoke without speaking. Hannah heard odd, quiet words over the distant peal of the bell, heard the coarse and unusual accent as the woman murmured a single sentence.

"Welcome to the Hotel Rojo."

* * * * *

In one of his many homes, Zin reclined in a leather armchair and strummed his guitar, driving out *Laredo*, only not as lovesick and smooth as it should have been. His rendition had an edge of longing, yes, but also anger and grief and absolute frustration. After all, the feelings had to go somewhere.

While I'm there I will sorely miss you, my love, how much I can never tell

And this golden key, now take it, my love, and open my secret heart;

How much I shall always want you, my love and how great my pain to part...

Through the ages music had been a part of his life, his very essence. From the ancient chants of his people, to mariachi tunes, to rock and roll—all wove through his centuries of existence like gold threads in a ceremonial garment.

Tonight, as he played the haunting modern melody, it brought back memories of a time long ago. He closed his eyes and images formed in his mind. Of Aki, with hair as dark as a desert night with the gloss of stars woven through it. A sensual woman with unusual green eyes spun with gold.

Aki, the woman who was to have been his Eternal Mate, but who had been murdered over five hundred years ago. She'd been his other half, his *alma*. His soul.

His heart had never healed since she'd died at the whim of the so-called Aztec gods. Still a virgin, she'd been sacrificed on an altar to appease the cruel "gods" who had virtually enslaved Zin's people. Without daily sacrifices, the creatures would terrorize the ancient city of Tenochtitlan. They would kill countless souls until they had quenched their thirst for the blood of weaker peoples, and assuaged their hunger for the hearts of strong warriors.

The fucking *Lopos*.

Even as he'd fought to get to Aki, her fearless golden-green eyes had met his and she had said, "I will find you again."

Zin had struggled against the warriors who'd held him back, but it was too late. The priests took her heart, and her blood had poured down the temple steps. Zin had wished to die with his woman, raged and roared and sworn his vengeance, even in the face of such bitter, horrid failure.

It was that night Creed had come to Zin with an offer he couldn't ignore. A proposition that would allow Zin to seek the revenge that had so quickly become his purpose. That very night Zin had given himself to the world of the *Vampiros*. He had chosen a life of immortality that would allow him to find his Eternal Mate when she came back to him, and to avenge her first death with the bloody fury he so desired to unleash.

Abruptly Zin opened his eyes. He slammed his palm down on the guitar strings to still them, to bring silence to the room. With a grunt of frustration, he settled the guitar against an end table and pushed himself out of his chair. A restless feeling overcame him as he strode to the bar in the corner of the great room.

The space was filled with heavy wood and leather furniture, tapestries with intricate Aztec designs, and items he had collected through the ages. The lighting was low due to his sensitive eyes, but he truly had no need for light. He was a creature of the dark — with dark responsibilities.

When he reached the bar, he ran his fingers through his shoulder-length black hair, then poured himself a double shot of tequila. He tossed it back in one swallow. The fluid burned the back of his throat and sent brief warmth through his body. Alcohol had no other effect on him, but he liked the taste of tequila. Especially the worm.

He smiled at the thought of Patricia, his outspoken live-in housekeeper. She always said he drank too much tequila for a vampire.

"All those worms." She always said this with a sniff. *"One day, you're gonna wake up and find a room full of pissed off worm-families. Dios. My poor fortune to work for a vampire drunk who can't even get drunk…"*

Zin poured another glass and carried it with him to the back patio. The double doors leading to the patio were open, and warm wind ruffled his hair. The hot breeze felt good against his bare chest as he moved onto the flagstone. He wore only black leather—an open vest, snug pants, and heavy boots.

He raised his glass and toasted the half moon. "*La vida buena*," he murmured, then sipped his drink, enjoying the flavor of the tequila as it rolled over his tongue. After a century or two he'd given up hope of finding Aki, and he'd turned his attention to killing all the *Lopos* he could find, and to living life fast and hard.

Dark responsibilities, dark passions.

Both were damned fun endeavors.

Unlike many other vampires he'd met over the centuries, Zin reveled in his immortality. He'd amassed a large amount of wealth, had traveled around the world multiple times, had learned countless languages and customs, and had seen history shape and reform, shape and reform. He fed off life, energy, art—anything vibrant and throbbing.

What wasn't there to like about living forever?

Except the *Lopos*, of course. The reason he had returned to Todos Santos yet again. And the fact that Aki was still lost to him, that he would never again know the joy of an Eternal Mate. Only for Aki would Zin have refused the immortality he so enjoyed. He would have been happy to grow old with her and to pass into the afterlife once they'd lived a full set of years.

"And don't forget the Solstice," he muttered, knowing the most dangerous time of year was fast approaching. In a few weeks, the seasons and the stars would change from spring to summer. At the turning point, the actual day of the summer Solstice, the *Lopos* would be at their most powerful—and their most desperate to collect as many strong hearts as possible so they might better attack the *Vampiros*. Maybe this year, the bastards would make a mistake in their frenzied "collecting."

Zin clenched his jaw. Staring out into the dark desert, he scented the Pacific Ocean blending with dry air, competing with the arid climate. Salt and sand. Dry breezes and wet brine. His was a world of contradictions, surely.

Contemplating this, he listened to coyotes howling in the distance, heard animal heartbeats that fueled his desire to feed. Soon it would be time to head into Todos Santos to slake his hunger by feeding on an unwary traveler or two.

But unlike the *Lopos*, Zin drank only as much blood as he needed, not enough to weaken his victim or to begin the process of transformation.

The *Lopos* preyed on all who came their way, human or *Vampiro*, or even poor desert creatures. If their human victim had inner strength or physical prowess, the *Lopos* tore out the heart and devoured it before the beat could stop. From weaker human victims, the *Lopos* took blood—too much, but not enough to finish the transformation—making a host of *sirvientas sangre*, blood servants, and sometimes one of the *Lopos'* many beasts. But if a vampire was taken, he was immediately turned into a beast, and his powers added to the collective.

Across the centuries, Zin and the extensive vampire organization—a coven of hundreds of *Vampiros*—had been fighting the *Lopos*. They had killed countless beasts over the years, but had yet to find a way to eradicate the most powerful. The "gods," as they would style themselves.

Zin downed the rest of his drink then slammed the glass on a stone patio table. *Enough. Time to feed.*

He strode through his sprawling home to the garage and flicked on the dim lights with his mental powers. His black Ferrari and his vintage red Corvette gleamed in the soft light. But what Zin most often chose to ride was the big chrome and black Harley-Davidson.

After he sheathed his long-sword in the bike's holster and armed himself with a small arsenal from the collection of weapons he kept on the wall, he opened the garage doors with a simple mental thought. Zin straddled the large Harley, and, with a roar of the monster's engine, he tore out of the garage. The door closed behind him with another mind command. After centuries of experience, his powers were great enough that his home was well-warded against intruders, even while he was away.

The engine thundered through the night as Zin guided the Harley toward Todos Santos and his evening meal. Cool air lifted his long hair from his shoulders and rushed over his chest and arms.

When he reached the bustling artistic community that had once been nothing but a tiny village, Zin parked the Harley just down the street from a local nightclub. In mere strides he slipped into the darkness of an alleyway, blending with the night until he found the perfect spot to watch, to wait.

Zin hitched his shoulder against the side of a building, listening to the pulsing beat of rock music coming from the club. It throbbed along with countless heartbeats. Ah, music. Nothing more mesmerizing—not even *Vampiro* mind talents. Zin knew he could lose himself in the stanzas for hours, letting them wind through his mind, curl across his flesh. Each note, like each heartbeat, had its own nuances.

While he watched the club, an unkempt drunk stumbled through its doors and toward Zin. But he ignored the man whose blood was far too tainted with alcohol. Beer—nasty stuff.

A laughing couple slipped out of the nightclub next, and Zin's hunger grew as he caught the scent of their lust, their blood, and the beating of their hearts. They'd had maybe a margarita or two and he wouldn't mind a little more tequila with his supper. Dipping into their thoughts, Zin learned they were both beyond horny. They could hardly wait to get back to their hotel room.

Well, darlings. I'll give you a little extra zing for your zip.

His incisors slid into his mouth as his oncoming prey drew near.

Using his mental powers, he lured them into the dark alleyway, away from flashing neon lights, until they were standing before him. Caught in his carefully cast entrancement, the couple ceased laughing and talking and merely watched him with complacent expressions.

"Hello, dinner," Zin said in a low rumble. "I promise, I'll leave you with more than I take."

Despite his well-wishes for humanity, this moment was always…delicious.

He gazed at his prey, battling the fierce rush of feeding-need. Their skin, so tan, like his own, but with the luster of pumping blood behind it. Humans always seemed so innocent, so naïve, even the worst of them. Their blood called to him in a feral blaze.

First, he feasted upon the man, sliding his fangs into the human's neck, and drawing part of the man's physical essence into his own. The rush of blood filled Zin's mouth and flowed down his throat, and he growled in satisfaction. The blood warmed his body, expanding through him, giving him strength and energy. He reveled in the taste, in the way the liquid essence exploded through his senses like a burst of lightning in a thunderstorm.

When he pulled away he licked the punctures, lapping up the last of the blood and healing the wound, leaving only two small purple marks.

"So much for the appetizer," he said, aware of the blood-husk in his words as he turned to the woman.

Ah, yes. Much better.

Zin knew many *Vampiros* made no distinction in their tastes, enjoying the sexual pleasures of male and female alike. He was built differently, however. Zin's desires extended to one gender, and one gender only. Each time he fed, he knew this truth all over again. Just looking at the woman, his cock throbbed hard against his leather pants. Nothing like female essence.

"Such beauty," he murmured as he pushed her blonde hair from her neck. "Come to me. Show me what you want."

He indulged himself a little, reaching just far enough into her mind to give her a taste of his sexual energy, of the pleasures he could offer her.

With a soft moan of ecstasy, she offered herself to him, begging for his bite, and then made a small mewling sound of pleasure as he licked the line of her neck, tracing the flow of her carotid artery. The drumming of her pulse pleased his tongue.

He thought about extending her pleasure as well as his own. He could bring her to orgasm with a tweak of the nipples, a brush of his mouth against her clit. She was ready. Zin could feel it.

But, no. This one belonged to another man, human though he might be. And Zin had never taken a woman unaware or unwilling—though he had enjoyed a few seconds of naughty pleasure like this.

Some other time, lovely. If you ever find yourself single, and in need…

Without further self-torture, Zin sank his incisors into the woman's warm flesh. He brought her soft body against his, enjoying the feel of her curves. It had been too long since he'd had a woman. Definitely too long.

Unexpectedly, while he drank his fill of his sweet prey's blood, Zin's thoughts turned back to the image of Aki. The vision grew stronger in his mind as he fed, only this time he could literally feel her presence, as if she was somewhere close by.

Impossible.

But he couldn't shake the feeling. He could picture Aki with her hair streaming in the wind, the glitter of stars in her golden-green eyes.

And she was driving a car?

Zin withdrew his fangs from his prey's neck and frowned. *What the fuck?*

Almost immediately, strands of *De Colores* twined through his thoughts. He could almost hear Aki singing it—but that was impossible. Aki had died centuries before the song was written.

No. This was something else. Someone else.

A feeling of doom rushed through Zin. He barely had the presence of mind to seal the wound on the woman's neck and give the couple instructions to return to their hotel room and fuck the hell out of one another.

The couple ceased to exist in Zin's mind as he turned his attention to the night. He could feel the woman's strength, her spirit, her fire. But he also sensed her sudden weariness and her need for sleep.

For a moment, he shared her vision, seeing the pulse of a red, red light.

Shit.

The *Lopos* had caught the woman with their spells and were drawing her to one of their lairs.

Fury and fear for this woman seared his veins. Was it Aki? How could it be, after all these years? Whirlwinds of excitement and doubt battled with his judgment.

He rose into the sky, his body parallel with the ground. With no thought beyond reaching the woman, he shot toward the Hotel Rojo.

He had to stop the woman before she entered the beasts' lair.

Leave now! he commanded her in thought. *Leave!*

The woman paused. She was linked with him. She did hear what he said!

And yet, he sensed her pushing away his command.

Zin doubled his effort to seize her thoughts, to make her heed his will.

She was stronger than any mortal he had ever encountered. She shook off his mental commands with almost no effort. That fast, her mind went blank to him. He lost any sense of her beyond the rising connection in his soul.

Gods! Will I be too late? Again?

Tensed, ready for war, Zin touched down at the end of the Hotel Rojo's long driveway.

A glimpse of long black hair and shapely curves was all he saw as the doorman followed the woman inside the lair and sealed it with a heavy thud.

Chapter Two
Night

Hannah shivered as the man closed the wooden doors behind her with a dull thump. Outside she had felt as if she was being watched, like something or *someone* was calling to her to leave the hotel. But as soon as the doors shut, the feeling vanished, as if the heavy wood had blocked everything out.

"I will park your car and bring in your bags," the imposing doorman said in a voice so stiff and so deep that it unnerved Hannah.

"Thank you." She handed him the keys with more than a little trepidation. It always made her feel uncomfortable turning the responsibility of her car and belongings over to a valet.

He gave a small bow and his hand closed over the keys. His dark eyes seemed to flash with a strange light before he turned away.

Hannah swallowed, hard. She resisted the urge to call after him, to tell him she'd changed her mind and wasn't staying here.

"You may call me Esmeralda," the woman said as she led Hannah away from the doorman and into the hotel's dim foyer. "Come, señorita, I will check you in."

"I'm Hannah Cordova," she responded as the woman continued to lead the way into an enormous lobby.

The woman gave no indication of hearing her.

Hannah paused. Taking a deep breath, she gripped her purse tight and gave her eyes a moment to adjust to the hotel's dim lighting. The lobby was richly appointed, yet eerie. More mosaics of Aztec gods graced the dark wooden walls, and couches and chairs of turquoise, orange and yellow were scattered about. Candles burned in wrought iron sconces around the room. The flames flickered and danced, drawing her back to the moment outside—

"This way," the woman said, bringing Hannah back to the present, away from the memory of her nightmares.

And then she swore she heard voices down the corridor echoing Esmeralda's earlier greeting, *Welcome to the Hotel Rojo…*

She gritted her teeth. *What's with you, Cordova?*

With a nod of her head, Esmeralda showed Hannah to the front desk where a large leather-bound book perched on the ceramic-tiled desktop. The older woman opened the old-fashioned guestbook and presented Hannah with a wooden pen from which blood-red feathers sprouted.

"Thanks." Hannah cocked one eyebrow at the quaintness of the guestbook and the strange plumed pen. She gripped the carved wood and then started to sign the page. Above the blank line she was about to write on were multiple signatures. Most had been written in a dark brownish-red ink, like dried blood. However, the last two lines were in bright scarlet, like fresh blood.

A shiver trailed Hannah's spine and she scowled at her silliness. She began to scrawl out her own signature and at once it felt like blood was being drawn from the tip of her finger. Her eyes widened and she swore she felt blood flow from her body through the pen and onto the book's parchment. She tried to stop writing, but the pen continued moving until her name was signed in vivid red.

Abruptly the pen loosened from her grip, as if demanding she put it down. Hannah's gaze shot to Esmeralda. The woman smiled—but her ancient eyes glittered with a strange light as she took the register book and the pen from Hannah's trembling hand. "It is a pleasure to have you stay with us at the Hotel Rojo, Señorita Cordova."

"Er, thanks," Hannah mumbled, resisting the urge to look at her finger. It throbbed like it had a hole in the tip. "Don't you need my credit card?"

"That will not be necessary." Esmeralda reached from behind the desk and brought out a fat candle secured in a ceramic candle holder. "You will pay later."

The candle wasn't burning, then all of a sudden it flamed to life faster than Hannah could blink.

How did she do that?

Grasping the candle in one hand and a heavy brass key in her other, Esmeralda gestured down a darkened hallway. "Your room, señorita. I will show you the way."

Hannah's finger continued to ache as she followed Esmeralda down the hallway. Almost afraid of what she would see, Hannah glanced down. A deep purple mark marred the pad of her index finger.

What the hell?

No. She refused to believe she'd just signed her name in her own blood.

* * * * *

Outside, still at the end of the driveway, Zin gave a frustrated growl and bunched his muscles, ready to charge after the woman and break into the realm of the *Lopos*.

You know you can't, came Creed's mind voice.

Zin cast a furious look over his shoulder at his friend and maker, who had touched down behind him. Creed's blond hair stirred about his shoulders as he eyed Zin with his intense gold eyes.

Like Zin he was dressed all in black, only he also wore a long black coat, concealing his weapons. Zin didn't bother to ask how Creed had known there was trouble. The beyond-ancient vampire was legendary for his keen senses and his ability to arrive wherever he was needed.

It's Aki, Zin replied in thought, *mi alma—well, her spirit at least. The woman I lost five centuries ago when I was still human.*

Your Eternal Mate. You're certain? Creed turned his golden gaze toward the warded wooden doors that kept the *Vampiros* from entering. *It would take incredible powers to open those doors to even one of us. Our combined strength would not be enough. Think, Zin. Before we take such a suicidal risk—are you absolutely without doubt?*

Absolutely. Another growl rolled up in Zin's throat. *You know I can't let them take her again.*

Aye. Creed's eyes met Zin's. *I'll send out the call. We need two more, old and strong. At least two more.*

Without waiting for confirmation, Creed's expression went slack. Zin knew he was using his powerful mind to summon *Vampiros* who could help their cause.

Still, Zin's black hair prickled along his scalp at the thought of leaving his Eternal Mate in the *Lopos* lair, even for another minute. If he could bypass the wards on his own, he would tear them down and charge inside. He'd give his blood, his heart, his head—whatever they would take or try to take—to save her.

But the wards were too strong. He knew without trying, and he knew he would forfeit the element of surprise if he acted like a passion-maddened idiot. Cooling desert air chilled his nose and throat as he brought his raging emotions under some semblance of control.

The bastard-gods would not begin the sacrifice until the rituals had been performed. That would take time, yes. Maybe enough, maybe not. Zin clenched his fists and bared his fangs.

The *Vampiros* had but a few hours to save his woman.

* * * * *

Esmeralda unlocked a carved wooden door and gestured for Hannah to enter. With a smile that didn't quite meet her eyes, the woman flipped on the dim lights and squinted. She set the old-fashioned key upon a table. "Enjoy a bath and relax, señorita. Then please, join us for a bit of dancing, perhaps some dinner."

"I'm not sure." Hannah pushed a heavy fall of her black hair away from her face. "I'm so tired."

"You could use a good meal," Esmeralda said as if the matter had been decided. "Join us in the courtyard when you are ready. There will be…music. You like music, yes?"

The woman turned and walked away, her sandals clicking against the tiled floor like bones rattling in the wind. Hannah closed the hotel room door and leaned against it, chiding herself again for her morbid thoughts. What was with her tonight? She usually wasn't one for an overactive imagination.

Well, not if you didn't count the vividness and clarity of her dreams and nightmares.

Hannah pushed away from the door and walked into the nice-sized room that was decorated much the same as what she'd seen in the other parts of the hotel. The only thing missing was a telephone. Oh, and no television. Other than that, much detail and work had gone into the room, probably to make the occupant feel welcome, but she felt more unnerved than anything else.

She rolled her eyes. "Get a grip, Cordova."

Shrugging off her uneasy feelings, she moved through the large sitting area to the bedroom. To her surprise, her suitcase was already laying on the large bed. That doorman was one hell of a fast valet. She tossed her purse beside the suitcase and kicked off her low heels.

For just a moment, her thoughts returned to the reasons she'd escaped Los Angeles. Timothy and his lies, the tabloids haunting her every move. It was a wonder she had managed to get away from California without being followed all the way here.

She bit her lower lip, hard, bringing tears to her eyes. *No, no, no!* She wasn't going to think about him any more. And no more stupid fears, no more being scared of her own shadow. She was an adult. She could handle what came her way.

The polished tile was cool beneath her bare feet as she stripped her clothing off and headed toward the bathroom. A nice hot shower was what she needed right now. The bathroom, like the bedroom, was also dimly lit, with a mirrored wall and a beautiful glass enclosed shower. When Hannah stepped under the warm spray she sighed with pleasure. The water washed away her fatigue and she felt invigorated and hungry for a good dinner as she soaped her hair and body.

Esmeralda had mentioned dancing, but Hannah had no desire to come that close to a member of the opposite sex. But the woman was right—she could use a good hot meal after all.

For some reason she didn't understand, she started singing *Laredo*, of all songs.

A love tune—well, a lost-love tune. The words sounded soulful and true in the shower, but Hannah pushed away her stirred emotions the moment she shut off the water.

Grumbling to herself about the stupidity and falseness of love, she grabbed a thick towel and rubbed herself down until she was dry. Her hair hung in wet streamers over her shoulders and down her back, and she hoped they had an outlet for her blow dryer.

When she stepped out of the shower she caught sight of her outline in the slightly foggy mirror. She rubbed the towel over the surface, drying it enough so that she could clearly see herself, naked and alone.

At that moment she visualized herself standing before her dream man, like she had in her night visions. If only he was real. He would wake her body, fill her senses, her mind, her heart.

Like the dream where the man was clad in a black leather vest and pants—while she was completely stripped of all clothing. She could just imagine running her fingers through his long, black hair, sliding her hands down his muscular chest and unfastening his leather pants to reveal a long, thick cock made for pleasuring her.

She sighed and brought her hands to her breasts as she watched herself in the mirror. She imagined her lover's hands and mouth teasing her instead. He would be so good, so slow, yet so powerful.

Someone she could love, someone she could trust.

Hannah brought one hand from her breast, over her belly, down through her soft black curls. While she continued to watch herself in the mirror she slipped her fingers into her folds. She rubbed her clit, imagining the man's fingers moving across the wetness instead of her own. With her free hand she pinched and pulled at each nipple, making them hard and harder yet.

It was unbelievably erotic, watching herself as she fingered her pussy and played with her nipples. She imagined her powerful lover watching her, commanding her actions with his gaze, his desire. The sensations in her body heightened. Would he enjoy sitting back while she stood before him and brought herself to orgasm?

Yes, he would.

He would stroke his cock while he watched her drive herself to climax.

Her gaze grew blurry as she drew closer and closer to completion. In her fantasy her lover would growl with satisfaction as she came. Even while her body was still trembling with her orgasm, he would bolt out of his chair, take her to the floor and drive his cock into her throbbing channel. He would fuck her hard and deep until she screamed her release—

Hannah's orgasm flared throughout her belly, shooting through her body like liquid fire. She watched herself in the mirror as she came, her body jerking against her hand, her skin glistening, her eyelids lowered and her lips parted.

Damn that felt good. So, so good.

And when the sensation faded, she felt even more alone than ever.

With a sigh, Hannah located an outlet then used her blow dryer to dry her hair, straightening the natural waves. She dug a clip out of her purse, gathered the thick mass, fastened it, and let it hang down her back. She touched jasmine perfume to each of her wrists and to the spot between her breasts.

After taking care of the basics, Hannah dressed in a white linen skirt that ended a couple of inches above her knee, showing off her long, golden legs. She chose a matching top that revealed her belly, along with the gold ring at her navel that glinted in the soft lighting when she moved. The ring had a jaguar engraved upon it, leaping toward a burst of light.

She slipped on a pair of white sandals and glanced one more time around the room. Now if she could only find a telephone to call Britt and let her know that she wouldn't arrive in Cabo until the following day.

After retrieving the brass key from the table where Esmeralda had left it, Hannah let herself into the hallway, closing the door softly behind her. After locking it, she slipped the heavy key into her skirt pocket. As soon as she turned from the door, an eerie feeling skittered along her spine — like she was being watched. She glanced up and down the dimly lit hall, but she was alone.

Let it be, Cordova. Chill out.

She headed back toward the lobby, but stopped when she heard music and voices. The sounds came from a passageway to the right that she hadn't noticed when Esmeralda showed her to her room. The music drew her, and she slipped into the corridor, walking until she reached an open pair of wooden doors that led into a small courtyard.

For a moment she stood in the doorway, watching dancers move to the music. The tune was strangely haunting, much like the song she'd been composing on the way to Cabo, before she ended up stopping at the Hotel Rojo. She couldn't tell where the speakers were—music surrounded them like it came from the night sky itself.

Men and women were dressed in everything from sparkling gowns and tuxedos to simple dresses and jeans. The evening summer air was warm, and a light sheen of sweat glistened on their pale skin. But what seemed strange to Hannah were the dancers' expressions. They were all similar—blank. As if they had no feeling at all.

Ridiculous, Cordova.

And yet she felt that deep, familiar pang of unfulfilled longing, and the abiding fear that she would end up like these dancers—going through the motions, feeling nothing. Being a star, finding her place in the world of art and music, those accomplishments gave her no assurance that she would be saved from such a fate. If anything, it made the horrible prospect more likely.

Blinking fast to drive back tears, she made herself look away from the flat, sweaty faces.

The cobblestone courtyard led to a building across the way. Torches burned on either side of an entryway at the top of carved stone stairs. It looked like an Aztec temple, and had dark brown stains running down the temple steps.

Stains like blood.

Hannah swallowed and turned her attention elsewhere, taking in the rest of her surroundings. Above them faint stars blurred across the sky, as if the air was somehow shrouded. Cacti and stone monuments crouched around the courtyard, along with torches on tall poles that illuminated the area with flickering orange-yellow light. The night smelled of desert air and burning pitch, and something...something almost *sinister*.

Three pale young men gazed at her through the moving crowd, motionless, glassy-eyed. Hungry-looking. They might have been handsome, if not for their colorless, listless stance.

"I am pleased you have joined us," came Esmeralda's voice from behind her.

Hannah nearly jumped out of her skin. She tore her eyes from the ghoulish boys, collected herself, and turned to give the woman a polite smile. "Everyone seems so subdued."

Esmeralda shrugged her broad shoulders, the jewels glistening in her hair. "Distraction can be bliss."

Before Hannah had a chance to respond, the woman moved into the crowd, toward a tall and imposing man standing on the other side of the courtyard, just below the temple. The dancers eased away from Esmeralda, as if they wished to keep a healthy distance, but they never stopped dancing.

Distraction can be bliss. What the hell had Esmeralda meant with that comment? With a frown Hannah studied the people dancing, and for an instant, she swore she could sense their despair, their loneliness, reaching for that well of tears in her own soul. From some she sensed the desire to go back to remembered times, and from others she felt the deep-seated need to forget, just forget.

Just like her. The need to forget her worries, to just join the dancers, flowed over her like warm water. As if she should just give herself to the swell and wash out to sea.

Hannah squeezed her eyes shut. God, was she getting morbid, or what?

"Something to drink, señorita?" Hannah opened her eyes to find a waiter standing before her, dressed much the same as the other hotel staff she had encountered, as if he were an Aztec warrior.

She certainly could use a drink. "A glass of chardonnay, please."

"My apologies." The man's expression was one of cool indifference. "Chardonnay is not on the menu. Perhaps some champagne?"

Doing her best not to frown, she nodded. "That's fine." She wasn't crazy about champagne, but whatever. She just needed a drink.

Feeling the need to just *do* something, she slipped through the crowd and headed toward the temple. Esmeralda and the man were no longer at the base of the small stone monument and intense curiosity filled her. Hannah slowly climbed several steps until she reached the top level that led to a large chamber. To the right of the chamber door was a reclining, bent stone figure that Hannah recognized from her ancient history studies. It was a *chacmool*, a figure that held a dish where Aztecs placed hearts cut from sacrificed victims as an offering to their gods.

At the sight, a sharp ache stabbed Hannah's chest and she held her hand over her heart as if to protect it. She shivered and shook off the feeling. Ever since she'd arrived here she'd been acting ridiculous, getting spooked over nothing.

Silently she slipped to the doorway of the chamber and leaned against the stone wall as she peeked inside. The chamber was enormous—much bigger than she had realized.

At the center of the chamber several people in Aztec garb gathered around a table and she couldn't see what was on it. She heard muttering in a strange language that she didn't recognize, although it sounded like some kind of ritual chant.

The people moved to the sides of the table revealing Esmeralda behind it, facing the doorway—but she changed before Hannah's eyes.

Esmeralda's face transformed into a hideous parody of an Aztec goddess, a skull at her waist, and her skirt—her skirt appeared to be made of living serpents. Serpents that wriggled and hissed.

Hannah felt the blood drain from her face as her gaze dropped to the tall slab of stone. It wasn't a table. It was an altar, like the one from her nightmares.

On the altar a naked man was strapped down. His muscles strained as he fought against his bonds, but he was too tightly bound. At his head stood the three colorless young men, clearly ready to restrain him if he broke free.

In her horror, Hannah barely saw the glint of a steely blade before Esmeralda plunged it into the man's chest.

Hannah screamed and bolted from the chamber. Her sandals slid on the stone floor and she tumbled down the steps below the temple, scraping her bare arms and legs. At the bottom she hit her head hard enough that bright sparks lit up behind her eyes. Her body shrieked with pain and her head ached, but she never stopped moving. She scrambled to her feet and bolted through the dancers, shoving them out of her way. She had to get out of there. She had to find the way back to the lobby and out of this nightmare.

Panic nearly overwhelmed her as she tore into the hotel and down the dim hallway. At the end she burst into the hotel's front lobby. Blood pounded in her ears and terror seized her insides.

The doorman stood before the wooden doors in his Aztec garb, his hands clasped before him, his legs positioned in a military stance.

"Let me out!" Hannah shouted as she dodged around him and reached for the door handle.

He grabbed her by her upper arm in a vise-like grip and jerked so that she was but inches from him. She suddenly saw him for what he was—not a man, but a beast. A misshapen head and long teeth that gnashed at her. A stench came from his mouth that nearly gagged her.

His voice was a low growl as he spoke, "You are ours, Hannah Cordova."

Chapter Three
Middle Night

A good hour after seeing the woman enter the *Lopos* lair, Zin was still pacing the end of the Hotel Rojo's driveway. He clenched and unclenched his fists. His instincts tore at him, demanding he say the hell with waiting and force himself into the building to free his woman—even though he didn't have enough power to do it on his own. When the other *Vampiros* arrived, they would have but moments to grab the woman and escape with her. They couldn't fight the *Lopos* with so few.

It maddened him to have to wait until enough members of the coven had arrived to combine forces and break the wards. But he had no choice. He risked the woman's life and his own if he charged in without thought.

Through mental commands, Creed had called to two more members of the local coven of *Vampiros*. Over 800 years old, a former knight in the Crusades under King Richard the Lionheart, the golden-haired Creed was the oldest vampire in the coven and had the farthest reaching mental powers, even stronger than Zin's.

Finally, when he thought he couldn't stand waiting another moment, two *Vampiros* arrived to assist Zin and Creed.

"A broad, eh?" Brandt landed nearby, his boots crunching stone as he strode toward them. Once a stockbroker on Wall Street, he had only been "made" twenty-eight years earlier when he was thirty-seven. Brandt was the youngest member of the coven, yet quite powerful. "This better be good, old man."

Zin let out a low growl and narrowed his gaze at the whelp. Brandt winked at him, enhancing the mischievous twinkle in his boyish blue eyes.

William walked up to the three, not making a sound. A former pirate, Will was just over 200 years old. He had his dark hair back in a queue and wore black jeans and a black tunic, loose at the sleeves. He folded his arms across his chest, a dark expression on his face. His long-sword gleamed at his side in the pale moonlight.

Creed turned to Zin and the other *Vampiros. Our powers can get us in through the Lobos warding,* he said, *but we will have to fight our way back. It is likely some of us will not make it.*

Brandt and Will shrugged. Zin snarled with impatience.

Well, then. Creed turned toward the Hotel Rojo. *Let's have at it.*

All the vampires focused their attention and their powers on the front doors of the *Lopos* lair.

Their minds joined as one, becoming a great battering ram, pounding again and again on the shimmering magical wards.

The wards gave a fraction.

Brandt laughed.

Will growled. *Let us at them.*

Focus, Creed instructed blandly.

They kept up their assault. The *Lopos* would know nothing as yet. It was clear their attention was elsewhere. No significant energy reinforced the wards as the four tore the magical bonds apart.

With great stealth, they lifted off and flew through the cool night air to the Hotel, each quietly touching down in front of the large wooden doors.

When he reached the doors, Zin paused, waiting for the combined strength of the four *Vampiros* to finish opening the warded door. Anger intensified his need to get his woman, to save her.

Your eyes will be my single shelter, he thought harshly, letting the music of battle, of sacrifice, ring through his thoughts.

This time, he would make it.

This time, by the strength of his many years of life, by the force of his *Vampiro* blood, he would not fail.

✳ ✳ ✳ ✳ ✳

"Go to hell." With all her might, Hannah jerked away from the hideous doorman-beast and pulled her arm free. His claws scraped skin from her arm and pain flared from the wound as she stumbled back.

The doorman-thing grunted. He seemed almost surprised.

Hannah pulled out her door key and wielded it like a knife.

In the background she heard the rush of feet over tile and shouts of several voices, and her heart thundered. "Just get away from me!"

The beast-man snarled and reached for her again, his claws barely missing her as she stepped back, brandishing the key.

"You *are* going to let me out of here," Hannah yelled, anger welling inside her. Anger at what she had seen. Anger at not being allowed to leave. Anger at all that had happened since Timothy had gone to the tabloids. Anger at what he had not only done to her, but to her sister and mother.

Blood from the claw marks rolled down her arm as she put her hands up, palms facing the beast as if to fend the bastard off. Along with her fury, an incredible sense of power built in her mind, so strong she had the sudden feeling of invincibility.

Beast-man made a noise of confusion, and the rushing of feet and all the shouts abruptly went silent.

"Can she?" someone asked in a thin, reedy voice.

"No," came Esmeralda's self-assured and sneering response. "Of course not."

Hannah ground her teeth. *Bitch. Bitch!*

She threw down the key. It clattered on the tile floor as she held up her hands, following an instinct she didn't understand. Light burst from her palms. From her entire body. An intense freaky blue light that caused Hannah to freeze in surprise, despite her rage. It was so bright she could barely see anything around her. Her body was on fire!

Without warning, her hair clip flew loose and exploded. At the same moment, beast-man screamed and staggered. More shouts and screams of pain came from all around her.

Hannah didn't stop to wonder what was happening. She dove for the door handle and yanked as hard as she could, ramming it against the screaming beast-man. Light still blazed around her and her body still felt hot.

She stumbled through the doorway, into the night, into the desert, to freedom—and slammed directly into a hard male body.

"Aw, shit." The man held one arm over his eyes, as if he couldn't bear the light coming from her, either.

Before Hannah had a chance to gather her thoughts and ram her knee into the man's groin, he grabbed her around the waist and threw her over his shoulder.

"Let me down!" she screamed and struggled against him. He whirled and ran from the hotel as she beat on his back. She saw more figures surrounding them, but the strange glow from her body seemed to make them back away, move, circle around her—and then they converged. The sounds of fists hitting flesh, swords hitting swords, and gunshots rang out.

Hannah fought even harder against the man who was holding her. Just as she was about to dig her nails into his back beneath his leather vest, she was suddenly horizontal. Flat on the man's back, half on him and half off.

They rose up into the air and then they were flying away from the hotel.

They were freaking *flying*.

"What the hell?" This time Hannah clenched the waistband of his leather pants as tightly as she could, afraid she was going to tumble to the ground—which was growing increasingly farther and farther away, as was the hotel. For that she was grateful, but her thoughts were too confused, too angry, too freaked out, to know *what* to think about everything that was happening.

Her heart still pounded furiously against her ribcage and her body trembled with fear and rage as she clung to his back, upside down, her thighs around his neck and her hands on his ass. The strange bluish-white glow vanished, and every cut, every bump and bruise on her body screamed with pain. Especially the claw marks from the beast-man—it was like hot coals had been inserted into the deep scrapes, and the feeling made her so nauseated that her head swam. Blood continued to flow from the wounds and dripped onto the man's leather clothing.

It was all so surreal. Like a nightmare, a waking dream that wouldn't let her go.

"Shhhh," the man was saying in a strangely calming tone. "You're all right now, *mi alma.*"

"Bullshit." Hannah gripped his pants tighter as she peeked over his side and watched dark desert speeding by. "I just witnessed a sacrifice, I got held hostage in a hotel by hideous creatures, glowed like a neon sign, and now I've been kidnapped by a flying man in leather."

The man chuckled, a deep throbbing tone, but then his voice grew serious, angry even. "I promise those filthy animals will never hurt you again."

Hannah frowned at the piercing ache in her skull before she remembered hitting her head when she tumbled down the temple steps. Somewhere along the way she'd lost one of her sandals.

Certainly nothing like Cinderella.

And this guy, what was he? Some demented nothing-like-a-prince?

She glanced down, and for the first time noticed what a fine ass was beneath her hands. What powerful thighs the man had.

She banged her head against his back and closed her eyes. *Flying. Riiiiight.* And she was thinking about his ass?

It was all a freaking nightmare.

But he sure smelled good. Like leather and a wild male musk.

God, she was losing it bad.

The next thing she knew they were dropping in altitude and then the man righted himself and landed soundlessly in a near crouch. She opened her eyes to see flagstone beneath the man's boots. She was hanging upside down again, her blouse up over her breasts and her skirt hiked around her hips.

The man slipped her from his shoulder and her nipples rubbed against his leather vest as she slid down. When her feet touched the flagstone, she was standing directly in front of him. In a movement so fast she was caught off-guard *again*, he trapped both her wrists in one of his big hands. She found herself pinned to his hard length, her breasts flattened against his muscular chest and her hands bound behind her.

When she looked up at his face, she saw he was absolutely gorgeous—and found that she was absolutely speechless. Long dark hair hung in waves to his shoulders, stirring lightly in the night breeze, and his face had no hint of stubble. He had high cheekbones, black eyes, and the look of a fierce warrior. He wore only a black vest over his broad, sculpted chest and snug fitting black leather pants—and if that wasn't a steel rod between their bodies, the man had an erection the size of a policeman's baton.

When her eyes met his again, the corner of his mouth curved into a wicked smile. *Talk about a bad boy. A real bad boy.*

Then it hit her—the man from her dreams. It was *him.*

She shook her head and closed her eyes. She was out of her mind. None of this was real. *He* wasn't real.

The man kept his grip on her wrists with one hand and with his other he stroked the curve of her jaw. "Yes, this is very real, *mi alma*."

Hannah trembled at the contact and opened her eyes. "Who are you?"

Zin paused as he studied the disheveled woman who smelled of jasmine and the sweet scent of blood. Aki. It was Aki...yet not. Her long black hair was in disarray, her white clothing dirty and torn. Blood rolled down the side of her face from a knot that had formed on her temple, she had scrapes on her cheeks, arms, and legs, and she was missing a shoe.

She was the most beautiful thing he had ever seen.

His gut tightened. He would slay the beasts that had harmed her.

He lowered his head and lapped at the fresh blood on her temple and groaned at the sweet taste of her. He wanted more, *needed* more.

The woman went completely still, but he felt the pounding of blood through her veins and the throbbing of her heart, and his fangs nearly exploded from his mouth. His cock was so hard it was a wonder it didn't ram a hole straight through his pants.

Forcing his lust aside, Zin dipped into her unguarded and frenzied thoughts. She was frightened and angry, and she intended to kick him in the *cojones* as soon as she could pull away, which caused him to smile.

And her name was Hannah.

Hannah.

"I'm called Zin." He finally answered her question as he trailed his fingers from her jaw to the pulse point at her neck. "And you are my other half, *mi alma*, Hannah."

"I'm not your soul and I'm certainly not your other half, you delusional jerk." She scowled and tried to wrench her hands away from his grip. She'd had enough jerks this week to last her a lifetime. "Let. Me. Go!"

Even though he'd rather feel her body tight against him, Zin released his hold on her. She stumbled back against the patio table and braced her hands behind her on the stone surface. He frowned at the blood flowing down her arm even as the sight made him hungry to taste her again. Why was her arm bleeding so badly?

Incredulous, Hannah stared at him for a moment then narrowed her eyes at the man who called himself Zin. What kind of name was that? With his bad boy looks, Sin would have been more appropriate.

Then it occurred to her that he'd called her Hannah. She gave him her fiercest glare. "How did you know my name?"

He shrugged. "I read it in your thoughts."

She rolled her eyes skyward and stared at the stars for a moment. Denial kicked in hard, trying to save her sanity. She told herself she'd been kidnapped by a delusional *and* psychotic jerk.

But how did light shoot from her hands, and how did Zin fly? And why was she covered in blood? Her head felt like it was going to explode.

She desperately wished she'd look up, see a microphone, and find out she was on one of those "Gotcha" shows, a high-tech version. That any minute now a guy with a microphone would jump out of the woodwork and say something really, really stupid.

Please don't let this be real. It's too bizarre. I just can't take anything else in my life right now!

"Listen. I just want my belongings back and I'm out of here."

"I can't let you go." Zin slowly shook his head. "The *Lopos* would kill you. This time they won't wait before they perform the ritual. Coatlicue will take you and strap you to the altar, rip your heart out, and eat it while you watch."

At the cold, hard words and the angry look on Zin's face, Hannah flinched. She felt as if she was being drawn through one of her nightmares. Bizarre faces staring down at her...loud chants...a vicious knife plunging toward her chest.

Her body began to tremble uncontrollably and she lost her grip on the table. The world spun, the stars swirling above, and a buzzing began in her head. She slumped forward, the flagstone rising up to meet her.

He caught her and cradled her to his chest. "You're in shock, *mi alma*." He swept her up in his arms and she didn't have the strength to fight him. The darkness closed in on her, everything growing blacker and blacker until a pinprick of light was all that she saw...and then nothing.

Zin gritted his teeth as Hannah passed out in his arms. She felt warm and sweet, and at the thought of what the *Lopos* had done to his woman he was ready to tear into their lair and slice their heads from their bodies.

Beheading was the only sure way to kill a *Lopos*, for they had shriveled hearts — damned hard to tear out of their bodies — and of course, they truly had no soul.

That was one reason why they ate the hearts of the strong, to nourish the part of them that needed a mighty warrior's power. They fed off the blood of the weak for sustenance, but could not last more than a few weeks without eating a warrior's heart or drinking the blood of a fierce predator, whether male or female.

Zin turned from the depths of night and slipped into his home, carrying Hannah. With his powers he shut the doors behind him, not stopping until he reached his bedroom and his bed. Easily cradling Hannah to him with one arm, he used his free hand to pull back the comforter and turquoise silk top sheet, then laid Hannah on the bed, resting her head on a soft pillow.

The room was completely dark, a necessity come morning's light. With a simple movement of his finger, a slender candle flickered to life on the nightstand beside the bed. For a moment he just stared at his wounded Eternal Mate. She looked like a fragile *muñeca* — a fine porcelain doll — that had been badly mistreated. Her blood covered his hands and his arms, and he was afraid she had lost too much of the precious fluid.

A growl rose up in his throat and he moved away from her to search out supplies to clean her wounds. As a vampire he had no need of such things, but a human woman would. Patricia, his housekeeper, always insisted on having first aid supplies on hand, and insisted on cleaning his wounds when he returned from battling the *Lopos*. It made Patricia feel better, more useful, so he humored her and kept a first aid kit. Now he was grateful for it.

Zin went into his bathroom where Patricia kept the supplies. He left the bathroom door open as he returned, dim yellow light spilling into his room from behind him. Hannah was still asleep, but she stirred and softly murmured something he couldn't understand, and her eyelids fluttered. First aid kit in hand, he sat on the bed beside her, the mattress sinking a little from his weight.

After he opened the kit and set it on the bed, he brushed the wild mass of hair away from Hannah's face and began attending to her cuts and scrapes. She had bled so much, everywhere. Carefully, he brushed a cotton ball saturated with antiseptic over her temple, and cleaned away dried blood crusted along the side of her face. When he'd licked the wound on her temple earlier, he had sealed it, stopping the flow of blood, and the wound was already beginning to heal.

While he attended to her his thoughts ran through the evening. Before he and the *Vampiros* had time to rush the *Lopos* lair, Hannah had bolted out the door and straight into his arms. Only she had glowed with an eerie light so bright that it had damn near singed his eyeballs. He'd never seen anything like it. Could this woman have some kind of power? The power of light? Was that how she had broken through the door's warding before Zin could?

Creed and the others might have some idea, but they were busy at the moment, dressing their own wounds in their various lairs. His powerful senses told him they had all escaped, but only because Hannah had escaped, wielding whatever strange power it was that she had. Otherwise, they would never have been strong enough to drive back so many rabid *Lopos*.

Zin gently searched her face and neck for wounds. He could only take living fluid; he couldn't ingest dried blood without becoming weaker. So it was necessary to cleanse away the old blood with antiseptic before lightly licking the scrapes to help them heal faster.

When he finished with her face, and neck, he started on her arms. One arm had no scrapes, but he stilled when he saw her other one. Blood oozed from wounds he couldn't see because so much blood smeared them. His fangs filled his mouth with the desire to taste her blood again, but at the same time fear filled his heart at what might be lurking beneath the red fluid.

Zin wiped away the blood from her arm with an antiseptic-soaked cloth and his gut clenched when he saw the three claw marks from one of the *Lopos*. Hannah's arm had been scraped so deeply that blood continued to flow from the scrapes and onto the silken sheets. He growled at the sight of the marks and clenched his teeth. Hannah moaned in her sleep and tried to pull her arm from his grasp.

The poison was working through her system even as she slept. And there was only one way to draw it out and save her life.

Without hesitation, Zin raised her arm to his mouth and sucked at one of the claw marks.

Vicious pain splintered his head as the poison left Hannah's body and flowed into his own. He narrowed his focus to the wound, forcing himself to ignore what was tearing his body apart. She would not survive the poison coursing through her veins if he didn't get it out. He had no choice but to try the most delicate of tricks, filtering her blood through his teeth without drinking anything but the poison, and sending her cleansed blood back into her body without a drop of his own essence.

It seemed an eternity before the *Lopos'* vile fluid was drawn from the first wound, Zin licked its length, sealing it shut so that blood no longer flowed. His head spun and his body grew weaker, but he had to continue. He would not stop until he had filtered every bit of tainted blood.

Hannah moaned again, tossing her head back and forth upon the pillow. Her face was pale against her dark hair splayed across the turquoise silk.

He brought her arm closer to his mouth even as she tried to pull away from him in her sleep. His fangs brushed her skin before he sucked at the second claw mark. Pain, even more intense, racked his body, stabbing at his chest. He ignored it, bringing out the poison, pulling it into himself until her blood and the wound was clean. He then sealed it with a swipe of his tongue.

Hannah's soft cry brought his attention to her lovely features again. Her eyelids fluttered and rose as if she was watching him. But no, he was certain she still slept, perhaps lost in some dream world or nightmare. He would have slipped into her mind to help rid her of any mental anguish, but he was far too weak from the *Lopos* poison. He *would* complete this task.

Zin didn't slow his efforts when it came to the third and deepest scrape. It felt like a thousand knives pierced his skull, his body. Harder and harder he sucked the claw mark, the evil flowing over his tongue and down his throat.

When he finally filtered out the last drop of poison from her blood, he shook so badly he had trouble sealing the wound. It took longer than it should have, for such a simple task.

Zin felt a flare of impatience, and that flare took what little energy he had left. He blinked at the now-healing cuts on Hannah's arm. They blurred. He frowned and gnashed his fangs. The room seemed to narrow, then blur like the cuts. Zin's head spun. Up became down, and down, up. He slumped over and slipped to the floor, unable to control his muscles.

Before he could even call for help, he faded from consciousness.

Chapter Four
Early Morning

"*Where are you?*" *The voice called as if from a great distance.* "*Where are my daughters?*"

Hannah soared through night sky and summer breezes. Her white feathers ruffled in the desert air, blissfully cool after the sun vanished beyond the horizon. The voice faded before she could recognize it.

Her vision was sharper now, clearer. Below her ran a black jaguar, a fearsome yet proud beast that seemed overly aware of her.

Guardian…or predator?

She dipped her wings, enjoying the freedom of flight and the peace of being alone.

Yet she wasn't alone. The jaguar haunted her every dip and dive, watching her with glittering black eyes.

Pain stabbed at Hannah's wing, swift and sudden.

Something vicious and unseen ripped her feathers and clawed at her body.

Hannah screamed as she fell from the air, her cry like that of an injured dove. She spiraled toward the ground — and toward the jaguar waiting below.

The huge cat opened his mouth and caught her before she slammed against the ground. She struggled to free herself but his jaws held her securely.

He kept running, not hurting her, simply carrying her.

A weight dragged her down, down, and farther down until darkness shrouded her.

Hannah's eyelids flew open as she woke from her nightmare. A nightmare that was almost like a dream-walk or a vision...

It took a full minute for her senses to shed the feel of the desert, the warmth of the jaguar's mouth. Gradually, she came to understand that she was lying in a dimly lit room. Her body felt weak and heavy as she struggled to a sitting position. Pain splintered through her head, and for a moment she paused, fighting back a wave of nausea.

After the urge to vomit finally passed, she managed to push herself up against the wood rail headboard. Confused and disoriented, she struggled to place where she was and why she felt like she had the worst hangover of her life.

Her head continued to ache as she battled to remember what had happened and how she came to be in this room she didn't recognize. The room was very masculine, with large heavy wood furniture and décor in shades of turquoise, desert greens, and browns. She was sitting on a bed of turquoise silk, and carelessly tossed aside was a comforter in the same colors as the room. The only light came from a bathroom to her right. Wherever she was, she definitely needed a bathroom, and now.

She braced her hand on the mattress and felt something stiff and dry beneath her palm. Almost afraid of what she would find, she glanced down at the sheet. A dark pool of brown stained the silk—like dried blood.

Her heart beat even faster and her gaze cut to her clothing. She was wearing one of her favorite outfits, yet she barely recognized it. More dried blood splotched it, and the blouse and skirt were both torn and filthy.

Hannah gulped back a sudden rush of fear. And then she saw the claw marks on her arm. Three of them. Deep and purple, yet not bleeding—already healing, in fact.

In a rush everything came back to her, so fast and hard she felt like her head would rupture from the pain. She held the heel of her hand to her forehead as everything sped through her mind. The hotel and signing her name in blood. The dancers, the sacrifice, the beast-man clawing her arm. Blue light bursting from her body, and flinging herself through the door and into the arms of a dark stranger. A man who had *flown* and brought her somewhere.

No doubt to this place.

And what? Left her to bleed to death or die of shock?

She put both hands to her temples and fought to gain some kind of control over the images. A nightmare. That was it, sure. Nothing had really happened, had it?

But if nothing happened, why did she have gouges in her arm? Why did her body ache and her head feel like it was splitting in half? Why was she covered in blood? The last thing she remembered was passing out and the dark stranger catching her.

Zin. He'd called himself Zin.

Oh, God, she was losing her mind.

Slowly Hannah raised herself from the bed and slipped her legs over the side. Her lone sandal slid off with a light thump on the tile and she vaguely remembered losing the other one. While flying?

Whether she was hallucinating or not, right now she had to pee so bad that her first priority was the bathroom.

She slipped off the bed and began to step forward when she stumbled over something on the floor. Something big and hard.

Hannah barely managed to keep from falling face first on the tile, landing instead on her hands and knees with an *oof*. The pain of impact only took her attention away from the rest of her aches for a second. She hurt so bad, what did one new little pain add to the rest?

She turned to see what she had tripped over and saw that it was a man.

Zin. And he was strangely still.

Feeling both afraid and curious all at once, she moved around on her hands and knees so that she could look down at him. Okay, so the bathroom *could* wait a couple of minutes more.

Damn but he was gorgeous. He had strong features, high cheekbones and deep set eyes. His hair was blacker than her own, the color of midnight, and he had a sinfully sexy mouth. His leather vest was open, revealing his great physique. He looked like a guy who lived at the gym. All the clichés rushed through her mind. *Sculpted chest, six-pack abs, muscled arms, buffer than buff.*

"So this is why they make clichés," she muttered.

Buff or not, she sensed Zin wasn't the pretty-boy type who worked out just to show off his body. He seemed harder than that, more seasoned. Her gaze trailed down his waist to his hips and his powerful leather-clad thighs, to his boots. Almost like some Spanish cowboy, or the warrior-king-in-disguise from an epic fantasy film.

Then her attention returned to his strange stillness. She didn't even see the rise and fall of his chest. He seemed a little paler than before, too.

Not knowing why she did it, Hannah put her cold fingers to his neck and her gut clenched when she didn't feel a pulse. Fear for him flowed through her, but she didn't know why. Wasn't this the man who had kidnapped her?

Or had he saved her?

The man's eyes snapped open and he grabbed her wrist so fast she yelped in surprise. He held her hand tight against his neck, his eyes intently focused on hers.

"Let me go." Hannah's voice trembled as she spoke.

Never taking his eyes from hers, Zin slipped his hand from her wrist, slowly moving up her arm to her elbow in a sensual caress that took her breath away. "*Mi alma*," he murmured in a low throbbing tone.

For that moment, Hannah was trapped in time. Her whole world narrowed to the man lying on the floor beside her. She'd never met this man before last night, knew nothing about him, yet she felt as though her soul had known him forever…and her heart knew him, too.

I could trust this man, a part of her insisted. *I could love him.*

Another part of her mind woke long enough to insist, *And he'll write about it all for* Star News *and* Tattler.

That jolted Hannah back to reality. She yanked her arm from his grasp and scrambled to her feet. "Zin, or whoever you are, just stay the hell away from me."

He smiled and then winced. "It's good to see you're doing better."

"Listen." She jerked her head toward the bathroom, causing more pain to explode in her head. "I've really got to go. When I come out, you're going to explain to me what the hell's going on."

Zin rolled onto his side and propped himself on his elbow. He grimaced, still looking pale, but he said, "I'll be right here."

With a sigh of frustration, she turned on her heel, went into the bathroom, and slammed the door shut.

Hannah headed toward the toilet but stopped when she glimpsed her reflection in the mirror. She looked horrible. She had lost her clip and her hair was wild and matted, her face pale, a giant purple goose egg blotched her forehead, and she was covered in scrapes and scratches. Yet they appeared to already be healing, as if it had been a couple of days, rather than hours, since she'd been injured. Even the pain in her body seemed to be lessening.

Her attention turned to the three purple gouges on her arm. She flinched and gritted her teeth at the memory of the pain and the flowing blood. But now it only ached a little, and the claw marks were fading remarkably fast.

What really happened to me?

And how am I healing so quickly?

Nature gave her bladder another insistent tweak, and Hannah didn't have time to think about it anymore. She had to relieve herself—now.

When she finished she sighed with exhaustion, looking longingly at the shower. It was huge, an adobe-looking wall stair-stepping down around the side in a circular pattern. Forget what's-his-name, she was going to take a nice, long hot shower and collect her wits before facing him again.

In no time at all, Hannah stripped off her ruined clothing and darted into the shower. The warm spray soothed her aches and pains, and relieved some of the stiffness in her muscles.

While she showered, Hannah's thoughts went over and over what had happened, from the time she had stopped at the Hotel Rojo, to this moment that found her standing under a shower in a strange man's house. Everything blended into a sort of dream, a collage of images that she would have passed off as a nightmare if she didn't bear the cuts, bruises and claw marks to remind her that it was real.

She might be a small-town girl turned reluctant star, but she was no fool. Hannah knew a battle when she saw one. For whatever reason, the freaks in that Hotel were aligned against the...heroes?...mutants?...who had apparently tried to save her just as she was saving herself. Why she was a pawn in their game—other than the wrong-place/wrong-time scenario—she had no idea.

She poured a small amount of an earthy-scented shampoo into her hair and began soaping it through. It smelled good, wholesome and soothing, like the bathroom, and the bedroom, too. This place didn't give her the shivers like that hotel—and Zin didn't give her the inside-willies like Esmeralda did, either.

She thought about his touch, the way he looked at her, so adoring despite the fact she looked like Medusa after a bad bar fight.

Could she really trust Zin the way her instincts insisted she could?

Hannah snorted before letting the water rinse away the shampoo.

"No trust, no way. Not after Timothy." With a sigh, she finished her rinse. Trails of bubbles ran down her chest and belly, crisscrossing her legs with white patterns. Right now she didn't have a choice but to go along with this Zin character. All her belongings were at the hotel, including her clothing, her purse, cash and credit cards. She was going to have to find a way to get as far from here as possible—maybe she'd call Britt in Cabo and have her drive up. Hannah didn't care about the car or her suitcase anymore. She just had to get out of here.

Almost without thought, she hummed through *La Paloma Blanca*, then caught herself on the first *Let us dance the* jota *together*.

No. No catchy rounds, no sentimental crap. I'm keeping a clear head.

When she finished taking her shower, she felt immensely better. The pain in her head had lessened and she felt more relaxed, although still wary.

She dried herself off with a towel from the rack beside the shower, then wrapped the thick turquoise cloth around her slim body. Her thoughts returned to Zin as she rubbed another towel through her hair. The man was good looking in a hard, dangerous sort of way. Yet the thought of how lightly he had caressed her arm, and the deep timber of his voice, sent thrills from her belly to her sex. She didn't remember ever feeling the way this man had made her feel, and she didn't even know him.

Hannah stood in front of the mirror and glared at her reflection. Damn it. How could she be thinking of this man in any way remotely sexual? She'd been hurt, badly, and she wasn't about to let herself be hurt again in any way, especially by some stranger who thought he could read minds.

A stranger already bringing the music back to her heart, making her want to sing fast, upbeat tunes. She wanted to write, to create—*oh, damn.*

Yeah, Zin was definitely dangerous. And dangerous was something she didn't need.

* * * * *

Zin stared hungrily at the bathroom door. He had just taken a quick five-minute shower, changed into clean leather garb, and was now back in his bedroom. The damn *Lopos* poison still ravaged his body, and he had the mother of all headaches. He would need to feed, and soon, to cleanse the poison from his system. Likely he'd end up having to take one of Patricia's damn blood remedies to hold him over until he could find a human to feed upon.

Whatever. It was more than worth it.

He folded his arms across his chest and imagined how Hannah would look now in the bathroom...completely naked. He heard the shower stop and imagined her drying off her body with one of his towels. He pictured her bare breasts—would her nipples be the deep rose of her lips, or dark as blood? Would her lower curls be as black as her hair, or would she be completely shaved?

If he focused hard enough, if he could get through the continued pain from the *Lopos* poison, he could easily see an image of her in his mind, as she truly was at this moment. But he respected her privacy and would leave it to his imagination to fill in the blanks. For now.

He was still staring at the bathroom door, wondering what was taking Hannah so long, when he heard Patricia's voice behind him.

"Since when do you bring a woman into your home—other than me?"

He turned to see Patricia holding Hannah's shoe in one hand and a kitchen towel in the other. Before he could react, she swatted at him with the towel and turned her attention to the unmade bed.

With the bloody sheets.

"*Dios, Mio!* What happened?"

"The *Lopos.*" Zin towered over the petite dark-haired woman who looked after his home, and in many ways, his heart. He had to struggle to keep his balance because of the poison-induced headache. "One of the bastards clawed her. That's why there's so much blood."

"But she's still alive." Patricia frowned and cocked her head toward the bathroom door as she looked at Zin. "That means you took the poison from her body into yours, didn't you?"

Zin shrugged. "Hannah is *mi alma.*"

A smile spread over Patricia's face. "That's wonderful! I've prayed and prayed you'd find a nice woman. But you would have done it for anyone. I know you well, *mi hijo.*"

"My job," he grumbled.

"Ha!" Patricia snapped her towel at him again. "Well, since she's staying, I should fix her a bit of breakfast. The kind humans eat."

* * * * *

After she finished finger-combing her hair, Hannah heard voices coming from the other side of the door. Out of curiosity, she pressed her ear close to the wood. She heard a woman say, "But she's still alive. That means you took the poison from her body into yours, didn't you?"

Hannah's skin chilled. She backed away and braced one hand on the marble countertop. Vague flashes of memory came back to her. Zin gently treating the wounds on her face and hands as she passed in and out of consciousness. She remembered seeing him lift her arm to his mouth and suck from the wound — and the expression on his face — as if it caused him great pain.

She'd thought it only part of a dream, but he really had done that. She raised her arm and stared at the gouges that now looked more like deep purple scars than wounds.

A knock came at the door, but Hannah ignored it, still trying to grasp the meaning of what she'd just heard. She couldn't wrap her mind around any of it. It was too much, all too much.

The knock came again, louder this time, but it seemed faint and far away.

In the next moment the door burst open and Zin was standing in front of her faster than she could blink. "Are you all right?" His voice was gruff, but his eyes were concerned.

She was so caught off-guard that she stepped away until her backside met the marble countertop. All she could say was, "Uh, yeah."

"You were so quiet. And you didn't answer when I knocked." He braced his hands on the countertop to either side of her and stood so close she swore she could feel his body through the terrycloth towel. His hair was damp as if he'd just taken a shower as well. He wore clean leather pants, boots, and a leather vest that was open, exposing his muscular chest. "I was worried you had passed out," he added in a husky tone.

Hannah gripped the countertop tighter. "Did anyone ever tell you that you're far too intense?"

He stared in surprise, then gave her a sexy smile. "Patricia, my housekeeper, says it all the time."

"She's right, you know." Hannah knew she should tell him to go, but a tiny alien part of her didn't want him to leave. Obviously the part with no common sense. "You really need to relax."

"With you in my home, I can think of only one way to release tension." He pressed his body closer to hers. Her eyes widened at the feel of his erection against her belly. He dipped his head down so that his mouth was just inches away from hers. So close that she could feel his breath upon her skin.

A new, giddy dizziness disrupted her thinking and reason. Her body responded past anything her brain intended. She looked up at him, took in his hungry possessive expression, and she wanted him to kiss her—this man from her night visions.

She must be in one of her vivid dreams, and he'd come to her again. So what if she felt awake? He looked like he always did when he came to tease her, to take her to the brink of fulfillment before he vanished.

Every time, she forgave him for disappearing, and every time he came back. As soon as she saw him, nothing existed but a deep primal need for his touch. In those moments, Hannah had no thoughts of the past, no dreams of the future, just the throbbing, hot sensation of *now*.

If this was madness, so be it. She'd be crazy long enough to enjoy herself, to enjoy the *now*, just for a little while.

Before she even realized what she was doing, Hannah raised her face and brushed her lips over her dream-man's mouth. He felt so much more real than in her night visions. Soft, yet firm and immovable, like a rock. Like a real, solid lover who would never leave her.

Zin audibly sucked in his breath as she tasted his lips. He growled, a rumble that rose up in his chest like a wild beast, as he brought one hand to the back of her head. Her heart leaped as he clenched his fist in her hair and pulled her roughly to him.

She thought about screaming, protesting, pushing him away, but he literally captured her mouth with his, as if staking his claim on her. His kiss was hard, deep and possessive. A soul-burning kiss that ravaged her like wildfire.

Hannah's entire body started to ache.

He smelled of soap, the outdoors, and sexy male musk that was more intense now than in previous dreams, and his kisses had never felt so tangible.

"This is crazy," she whispered as he pulled back a fraction. "I'm dreaming. I always dream about you, and you always leave."

Her dream-man, or Zin—the real man who had somehow helped save her from real monsters—gave another rumble. Pleasure? Possession? She couldn't tell. She didn't really care, because he kissed her again.

"Those were no dreams, *mi alma*," he said when he at last released her, in a tone so low each word sent shivers up her spine. "They were visions of truth. It's common to dream about your true match, your soul's partner."

"But I have nightmares, too," she managed to stammer.

"Visions," Zin corrected. "I'll help make sure the bad ones never come true."

Another kiss followed, long and toe-curling. Hannah raised her arms, wrapped them tight around his neck, and slid her fingers into his long black hair, twirling her fingers in the wet strands. Vaguely, she realized the towel was slipping from her body, but her head was spinning from the kiss and she couldn't release him fast enough to catch it. As the cloth fell away, she felt the rough brush of leather chafing her nipples and the juncture of her thighs, and it made her want him even more.

Without breaking the kiss, Zin grasped her legs and raised her up so that her bare ass was on the cool, marble countertop, and his leather-clad thighs were pressed hard against the curls of her pussy.

God, how she wanted him, this man who had rocked her dreams for so long. She knew it was him. Knew it with everything she had, everything she was. This was the man who had come to her night after night, chasing away the nightmares and feeding her heart and soul.

He wasn't a dream any more. He was *real*.

"*Mi corazón*," Zin murmured as his lips moved from his Eternal Mate's mouth, down the line of her jaw, to the pulse point at the curve of her neck. "*Mi alma*."

He heard the beating of her heart and the rush of blood in her veins, and it made him hunger for her beyond rational thought. His mouth brushed over her life vein and he wished to slide his fangs into her skin and feed off her sweet blood at the same time his cock slid into her slick core. She would beg him for it—want him to fill her like no other man could.

He was still weak from the poison, but somehow Hannah gave him strength merely by her presence. If only he dared take her blood—draw it into his body—he could fully recover. But he wouldn't take from his Eternal Mate until she gave herself freely to him.

She tilted her head back, as if offering herself to him, even though she had no idea what he was. She wanted him. He could sense it, hear it in her thoughts and her soft moans, feel it in her pounding heart, and smell it upon her skin.

But what would she think when she found out what he truly was?

It didn't matter. She was *his*. She was strong enough to face the truth. She had to be.

Zin growled, a low throbbing sound that caused Hannah's body to quiver. All her aches and pains vanished.

He grasped her ass in his hands and pulled her more firmly against his leather-covered cock, and she wished there was nothing between them. He brought his mouth back to hers and kissed her even harder. Her tongue tangled with his and then lightly scraped his teeth—and his *fangs*?

Hannah jerked away, breaking the kiss. His eyes were heavy-lidded and he was breathing hard as he watched her, a sensual smile upon his lips. And he had fangs. Honest to goodness *fangs*.

"You're a vampire." She slid her hands from his neck and placed her palms against his chest, trying to push him away. "A freaking vampire."

Chapter Five
Morning

Zin shrugged his broad shoulders and gave her a wicked smile, exposing his fangs even more. "So I'm a vampire. What are you going to do about it?"

Hannah ground her teeth and shoved with all her might. "Back off. Now."

He didn't budge, just gave her that maddening, possessive look.

Great. Now, not only was she freaked about him being a vampire, she was really pissed. But along with anger came that feeling of power she'd had in the hotel, that feeling of invincibility. Her palms began to glow. Brilliant bluish-white light flared in the bathroom, and heat burned along her skin. The ring at her navel felt hot as molten gold.

"Damn." Zin staggered back and put his arm across his eyes. "Okay. Okay. Enough with the lightshow already."

Hannah's heart pounded as she looked down at her glowing naked body. What was happening to her? Even her nipples burned with fire, like little neon lights.

I'm losing my sanity. Maybe my body is possessed by aliens. Whatever. There's a real live vampire in here, and I've got to get out.

She scooped up the towel and darted from the bathroom before Zin had a chance to stop her, while she was still glowing.

There was just one problem. She had no clean clothes, and she didn't know where to run. Hannah couldn't sustain her anger. She felt too freaked out, and too confused.

Zin held one hand up, shielding his eyes as he followed her into the bedroom. "What the hell is with the light?"

The glow from Hannah's body faded to nothing, and her fear rose up again as she wrapped the towel tight around herself. "Just stay away." Her gaze darted around the room looking for anything that she could use as a weapon. That vase, or maybe the guitar...

Guitar?

"Not the guitar, all right?" Zin lowered his hand to the bridge of his nose and squeezed his eyes shut before opening them again. "Throw anything you want at me but not that. Please."

Something in his tone surprised Hannah—something she recognized. The man—the *vampire*—talked about the guitar like it was a pet, or a friend. Something alive.

Her gaze returned to him and she blinked. "You play?"

He raised an eyebrow. "Any better reason to keep a guitar around?"

She kept the towel wrapped tight around her as she glared at him. "That's just wonderful. You're a sarcastic guitar-playing vampire."

The corner of his mouth quirked. "And you're a cute little light bulb."

The mischievous glint in his eyes made her want to laugh. Absurd, considering she'd just discovered she'd been kissing a vampire—but he was right. She kept turning into a light bulb at odd moments.

And the fact that she accepted it so easily, that she truly believed he was a vampire and that she had developed the ability to glow, was beyond weird. But after all she'd been through since last night, anything was possible.

Trying to think of her next move, she shook back her hair. Wet strands brushed her bare back and made her shiver. "Do you have anything around that I can wear?"

A dark, sexy grin curved the corner of his mouth. "I rather liked what you were wearing in the bathroom."

Hannah reached for the guitar and Zin held his hands up in a gesture of surrender. "Okay, *mi alma*. I have a shirt around here somewhere, no doubt."

She watched him with a wary eye as he opened a bureau drawer. "How do you do that light thing?" he asked as he tossed her a black T-shirt.

Barely keeping the towel around herself, she caught the shirt with her free hand. "It's one of many talents, so just keep your hands and fangs to yourself, Mr. Vampire."

She wasn't about to tell him that it had never happened before last night. And she didn't understand it one tiny bit.

"So, last night was the first time?" He gave her that teasing look that made her want to deck him. "Quite a talent when it comes to the *Lopos*."

Hannah gave him her fiercest glare. "And vampires, too, apparently." She wanted to march into the bathroom to put the shirt on, but he blocked her way. "If you're not careful I might just flare up again."

He hitched one shoulder against the bureau and studied her. "It's something you have no control over. It's only happened when you were frightened for your life, and when you were frightened because I'm a vampire."

"I wasn't frightened of you." She clenched the T-shirt in her fist. "I was pissed because you wouldn't get out of my way."

"Frightened *and* angry." He folded his arms across his chest. "Both times."

Hannah wanted to throw her hands up in exasperation but she was afraid the towel would slip off. "Just get out of my way so I can get the damn shirt on."

His expression turned sensual, his black eyes smoldering. "I've already seen you naked."

"Fine." She glared at him and let the towel drop. The sudden rush of cool air against her nipples caused them to tighten. A rush of heat between her legs nearly made her groan, just like the flare of hunger in Zin's eyes. His response was immediate, unequivocal, undeniable—as was the bulge in his leather pants.

With great satisfaction she slipped the T-shirt over her head in slow motion, showing him exactly what he *wasn't* getting. It struck her then that she knew he wouldn't take it by force, either.

Damn. Even when she was trying to torture him, she trusted him.

It's not trust. It's insanity. Forget it.

She wriggled the T-shirt over her head, letting her breasts bounce with her movements.

"You enjoyed that, didn't you?" Zin's guttural whisper seemed to fill the room.

"Yes, actually, I did." Hannah managed a smile despite her traitorous body tightening at the sound of the vampire's voice. "I'm a performer. I like being watched."

Zin's heavy-lidded gaze didn't falter. "Bullshit. You talk big. Inside, you're a quiet woman with a quiet heart. Quiet, and loyal, and peaceful—but very, very passionate."

Hannah's eyes widened despite every attempt to maintain a disinterested façade. Had he grabbed that from her thoughts?

Just how much did this man know about her?

About my heart…

The thought nearly made her shake.

"Are you frightened, Hannah?" Zin's half-smile revealed the tips of his fangs. "Don't you think it's a bit foolish to tease a vampire? To toy with something you don't understand?"

Hannah's self-assurance faltered. His tone, so deep, so commanding, kept her nipples hard inside the T-shirt. Her pussy tingled.

"I-I'm not afraid," she managed. "That you'll hurt me. Physically, I mean."

"I'll never hurt you, no." Zin's expression darkened. "And I'll kill anyone who does. I can be a killer, Hannah. You should know that."

Hannah's breathing turned ragged. She thought about running, but she didn't really want to get away. No matter what Zin said, she sensed his goodness, the true light of his character.

That, or she was secretly suicidal.

In the space of an eye blink, Zin moved to stand before her. She gasped and tried to step away, but he grabbed her wrists in one hand and backed her up against a wall. He was so fast, so strong, yet graceful and gentle at the same time.

With just enough force to keep her helpless and excited, he pinned her arms over her head and pressed his full length against her. Fluttering sensations scattered throughout Hannah's belly. No fear, no anger. Just outright excitement. Zin's arousal was hard against her, his powerful chest nearly crushing her breasts between them.

"I wonder…" He sniffed at her wet hair and lightly brushed the wound at her temple with his lips. "With your hands bound, do you still have the power to glow like that?"

"Do you really want to find out?" she asked, making a half-hearted effort to sound unaffected by the way he was touching her. "Maybe this time I'll blind you."

His lips moved to her ear. "Would you want that, *mi alma*?" His tongue flicked over her earlobe and she barely suppressed a moan. "Or would you prefer me to see you, every inch and curve?"

Before she could answer, his mouth moved to hers and she pressed her lips together, fighting the urge to open her mouth and let him in. He gave a soft laugh and lightly bit her bottom lip. Hannah's lips parted on a moan and he took the opportunity to slip his tongue in. Gently but firmly he kissed her, drawing her in until she couldn't help kissing him back.

All the while, Hannah remained overly aware of her position. Zin still had her pinned up against the wall, her arms overhead, as if he'd taken complete possession of her. No man had ever done that to her—and she would never have imagined liking it.

With this man, she did. More than she wanted to admit. She stopped fighting his lips, losing herself in the sensation of his claiming kisses, his exploring tongue. The feel of the wall at her back, her arms raised high and helpless, her body barely covered and completely open to this dangerous, sexy being—it would have been enough to make her crazy, if she hadn't already lost her mind.

Zin kept his lips hard against her mouth. He slipped his leg between hers and pressed against her bare pussy, making her ride it. Hannah groaned at the feel of his thigh against her folds. She ground into him, rubbing her clit, trying to assuage the need building at her center.

He gave a low rumble of male approval, of pleasure. Hannah sighed as he slid his mouth from hers and he slowly pressed his lips along her jaw line. "You are so beautiful, *mi alma*," he murmured as he kissed her soft flesh. "Your skin is so sweet. I can't wait to taste all of you."

With a moan of surrender, she relaxed into the moment, wanting to completely give herself to this man. Something about him called to her in a primal way, deep and fierce—like she'd never known before.

Like her dream man.

He brought his mouth down to the hollow of her neck and flicked his tongue out, causing her to gasp with pleasure. He moved to the curve between her shoulder and neck and lightly nipped her. She felt the brush of his fangs—

"No!" Hannah jerked her neck away from him, the best she could with her arms pinned over her head. "Don't you dare bite me, you bloodsucking son of a bitch!"

Zin sighed and raised his head so that he was looking down at her. A hint of amusement played on his lips. "I would never take your blood without your permission. You are *mi alma*, my soul. Soon enough, you'll give yourself to me willingly."

She glared at him. "That's not going to happen. Not—not for biting, anyway."

Zin rubbed his thigh up against her pussy and she couldn't help the groan that escaped. "You want me."

Cripes. He was so handsome she could hardly take her eyes from his face. His long, thick black hair, those high cheekbones, the aristocratic nose, the firm line of his jaw, all those muscles so clearly seen beneath his open vest...*damn*.

"Whatever." Hannah did her best to collect herself. "That doesn't mean I want your fangs in my neck."

Zin drank in the smell of his woman as he brushed his mouth over her forehead. The need to taste her essence crested and broke, crested and broke. He had to claim her, had to have all of her. Louder and louder he heard the pounding of her heart, the rush of blood through her veins. He could smell her arousal like heavy perfume, clouding his senses.

"You will want me in every way, *mi alma*. That much I promise."

"Like hell—"

"Breakfast is ready for the señorita," came a woman's voice from behind him. Zin growled with frustration, but instantly released Hannah's wrists.

She dropped her hands to her sides.

He turned to his housekeeper and shook his head at her untimely arrival. "Thank you, Patricia."

Hannah slipped around him, her head raised high and her hand held out as she walked toward Patricia. Hannah was clad only in his T-shirt, which nearly dwarfed her, but she acted as if she wore a gown from the finest dress shop. "I'm Hannah Cordova."

Patricia took Hannah's hand and squeezed it between both of hers. "Of course you are, *mi hija*. You have the voice of angels, their many songs on your tongue, and in your heart."

Zin frowned. What the hell had Patricia meant by *that*?

But Hannah simply smiled and said, "*Gracias*." And then, "You look familiar. Have I met you before?"

The housekeeper frowned, then said, "Ah, no. That I would remember."

Still weaker than he realized from the *Lopos* poison, Zin held his fingers to his forehead for one moment. Just being with Hannah, desiring her so much, had given him a strange sort of high, an energy that had pushed away the pain.

But now he needed to feed. Needed to regain his strength.

He followed behind as the housekeeper led the way through his large home and into the spacious kitchen. Mahogany cabinets and ebony appliances gleamed in the soft lighting, and the granite countertops were pristine, as usual. The windows were well covered, the shutters blocking out the light.

There Patricia insisted Hannah sit at the breakfast nook while she was served a breakfast of *chilaquiles*, *tortillas* with *verde* sauce, rice, beans, and mango juice.

"My favorite." Hannah took a bite of the *chilaquiles* and closed her eyes in apparent bliss. "*Mi madre* used to make breakfasts like this."

Zin leaned one hip against a counter and studied her as she opened her eyes and turned her attention back toward the plate. At the mention of her mother she'd looked unsettled, but her features quickly returned to smooth and relaxed. For a woman who had been through hell and glowed like a blue light bulb, not to mention a woman who had just found out she'd made out with a vampire, she was amazingly calm. Only the trembling of her fork gave away her nervousness.

He enjoyed watching her eat, seeing the fork pass between her lips and the movement of her mouth as she ate. His gaze trailed to her neck when she swallowed and he became

73

transfixed by the vein pulsing at the base of her throat. The sound of her blood throbbing in her veins filled his senses and he could almost taste it.

When Hannah took a sip of her mango juice, for a fraction of a second, her gaze met Zin's. He gave her a slow smile, telling her without words that he intended to pick up where they left off at the earliest opportunity.

"Drink." Patricia interrupted their silent communication by handing him a glass of fluid that looked like a bloody Mary, minus the celery stick. "You'll need this to combat the *Lopos* poisoning. Until you go to Todos Santos to feed."

From the corner of his eye, he saw Hannah wince at Patricia's comment.

With a grimace, Zin took the glass. It was a strange concoction of spices and herbs, mixed with frozen human blood gathered from willing donors for emergency purposes. The only redeeming quality to the mixture was the shot of tequila that Patricia grudgingly added.

In one swallow he downed the crap, shuddered, and set the glass on the countertop. That fast, the brew started doing its work, giving him strength and endurance that would tide him over until he reached Todos Santos and found a few more...willing donors.

"I need to sleep—alone for a bit—and then I do have to go out early this evening." He caught Hannah's eye again. "Don't try to leave before I return. It's too dangerous for you yet. The *Lopos* aren't accustomed to losing their prey, and no doubt you saw far too much for their comfort. Best to give them time to turn their focus elsewhere. With the wardings around my home they won't be able to find you here."

She glared at him, but Patricia patted his shoulder. "I'll see to your woman, and you know it. Go, now. My magic is only human, so it won't last long. Rest, so you'll be at your best tonight."

With a curt nod, Zin turned on his heel and headed out of the kitchen toward one of the back rooms. He'd take a nap there, leaving his room free for Hannah in case she wanted to use it. His lips curled. He rather hoped she did—but, he'd wait. As soon as the sun set, he'd go back to the village, slake his thirst—and he needed to get his damn Harley.

Patricia could handle things until he got back.

If things like Hannah Cordova could ever truly be handled.

Hannah watched Zin step out of the kitchen and head down the hall. She grimaced again at the thought of him going off to suck on someone's neck tonight. It just seemed *wrong*. Did he kill the people he drank from? The thought sat poorly in her belly and suddenly she wasn't hungry for food. She pushed her plate away and looked up to see Patricia watching her.

"He is a protector of humans, not a predator," Patricia said with a knowing smile. She slid into the chair opposite Hannah and she caught the housekeeper's scent of warm vanilla and brown sugar. "Yes, he is a vampire, but he's a good man."

Frowning, Hannah stared at her juice glass, trailing her fingers up and down, through the condensation. "This is all too unreal." Her gaze returned to Patricia's. "Vampires and beasts? These things don't exist in the real world."

Patricia gave a soft laugh. "This is the real world, *mi hija*. The *Vampiros* keep humans like you safe from evils that would otherwise take over the 'real world' we talk about so freely." The woman gestured toward the rapidly healing wounds on Hannah's forearm. "If not for Zin, you would have died. I think you know that."

Swallowing back a rush of fear at the memories, Hannah nodded. "I remember it, yet it seems like a nightmare." She released the juice glass and clenched her fist on the tabletop, the image of the sacrifice dancing before her eyes. Most of all, she saw the three pale young men, holding the victim down.

Something about the memory of those three was particularly horrible. "It *is* a nightmare."

With a shake of her head, Patricia said, "Not any more. You are safe here."

"Really?" Hannah released a long shuddering sigh. "After this past week, I feel like nothing in life is safe or sane."

"Believe me, I understand." Patricia patted her hand and smiled. "Before I came here—well, I often felt the same. You will feel stronger and braver after more rest."

Instead of arguing, Hannah asked, "Where am I?"

"We're just outside of Todos Santos, far enough away from Hotel Rojo that you need not worry so long as you stay inside until they forget about you."

Hannah shuddered at the mention of the hotel. "Are you Zin's mother?"

"I'm his live-in housekeeper," Patricia said, "but he is like a son to me."

At the thought of how quickly Zin obeyed the petite woman's commands, Hannah smiled. He certainly hadn't argued over being told to bring her to breakfast or to drink that bloody-looking stuff. She grimaced at the mere thought of what must have been in that glass.

Before her stomach got any queasier, she turned her thoughts to other things. "How long did I sleep?"

"You slept the night through." Patricia stood and gathered Hannah's breakfast plate and juice glass. "But I think you should go back to bed. You've been badly wounded and you need to allow your body time to heal."

Hannah felt the exhaustion to her bones, but she didn't want to admit it. She needed to get to Cabo to meet with Britt.

Britt!

"Crap." She looked wildly around the kitchen. "I need a telephone. My friend will be worried sick about me."

"Of course. I'll take you to Ops. It's the only room here with a phone. Zin and I—we just don't like all that ringing."

Ops? What the hell is this? Spy vs. spy?

Patricia ignored Hannah's amazement and led the way to a nice sized octagonal room, pointed to the telephone, and left Hannah to make her call after giving her instructions on how to obtain the number to the hotel. She gave no dire warnings about keeping secrets or not trying to "escape."

Hannah realized she hadn't even considered telling anyone about Zin—and since the kiss they'd shared before breakfast, she hadn't thought about running away, either. What sense would that make, finally tracking down her dream man and leaving before she followed where her luck led? No way. She would stay, at least for a little while. After she called Britt, of course.

Before Hannah lifted the receiver, she stared around the unusual room.

The place seemed to be made of stainless steel, computer gadgets, and what looked like state-of-the-art communication and surveillance equipment. In fact, if she hadn't known better, Hannah might have thought she'd stumbled into an FBI field office. She had to smile. She had no idea what most of the things were, but it never occurred to her that vampires would be so…high-tech.

"That's Bond," she muttered. "Dracula Bond. Vampire Spy. Didn't you know?"

Giggles threatened to explode, but Hannah fought them back. If she started laughing, she wouldn't stop until Zin and Patricia had her carted away. Instead, she made herself dial the Vampire Spy's telephone and ask information for the number of Britt's hotel in Cabo.

When Hannah finally got herself patched through to Britt's room, her friend picked up the phone at once with an anxious, "Hello?"

"Hi, Britt—"

"Hannah?" Britt interrupted, her voice rising with obvious concern. "Where the hell are you? I've been standing by the phone, trying to track you down and waiting to see if you'd call. I've been worried sick!"

"I'm sorry." Hannah gripped the phone tighter. "I ran into a little bit of trouble."

"God dammit, where are you?" Britt's voice switched into ultra-panic mode. "What happened? Are you all right?"

"I'm fine. I'm not too far away, in a town called Todos Santos." As she spoke, Hannah searched the base of the cordless phone to see if there was a number she could give Britt. She found nothing. "I'm fine. I'll explain everything later."

"Hannah, this isn't like you." Britt paused before adding, "It's about that asshole Timothy, isn't it?"

Amazingly enough, the mention of Timothy's name didn't even faze Hannah. After all she'd been through, that wormy son of a bitch seemed like a mole on somebody's backside. But she didn't want Britt to worry more so she just said, "He's history and I'll survive. Don't worry, K?"

"Give me the number where you're at."

Hannah checked the phone base again. "I'll have to get it for you — I'm not sure what it is."

"You're driving me crazy, you little shit!" Her friend sighed. "Call me tomorrow. I'll kick your ass if you don't."

Hannah tapped her finger against the desk. It smarted, and she noticed the red mark on the tip appeared to be blistering. Not a big blister. Just a tiny, round, pinprick of redness. "I promise," she replied absently.

"I swear I'm coming after you if I don't hear from you by tomorrow evening."

After promising to be safe and call tomorrow for at least the tenth time, Hannah was finally able to hang up the phone.

She made her way out of "Ops" and wandered through the house. Almost in a daze she took in the furnishings, the dark polished woods, the ancient artifacts scattered throughout the living room and the rich oil paintings adorning the walls.

Even though the house was enormous, it wasn't long before she found the bedroom where she'd spent the morning. The bed was newly made, and all Hannah could think about was crawling beneath the covers. Her limbs felt heavy, her eyelids drooped and her body succumbed to exhaustion.

Giving in, she did crawl into the bed, and straight under the covers. Silk sheets rubbed softly against her battered body, soothing away her fears and tension. In minutes, sleep claimed her.

Chapter Six
Night

Zin slept for half the day, then spent the afternoon in Ops monitoring his scanners, dozing a little more, and checking on Hannah while she grabbed a siesta of her own. She looked so peaceful as she slumbered, so beautiful, the stuff of paintings and statues. How had he been so fortunate, to have the opportunity to claim such a woman — again? Zin bared his fangs. Time to make sure his strength was full-force.

After slipping into the garage and arming himself as usual, Zin flew through the dark sky toward Todos Santos. His mind was consumed with Hannah. Her touch, her smell, her taste. She reminded him of his Aki, looked so much like her. Yet Hannah was different, and she intrigued him in ways that even he couldn't fathom.

Was it possible Hannah was an even better match for him than Aki had been? Could his second chance at love prove more rich and inviting than the first?

The very thought boggled his mind — which was already boggled enough. Flying weakened him further, and he knew he had to feed — and soon. The *Lopos* poison still flowed through his veins, and only untainted blood would return all his powers and his full strength.

Warm desert air flowed through his hair and over his bared chest. The night smelled of an oncoming desert monsoon, sure to arrive soon. But something else was on the wind...something evil. Zin couldn't track the scent in his weakened state, but he knew it warranted concern.

When he reached the village, he landed in a crouch near the Harley that he'd abandoned last night. As he'd expected, the bike was untouched, the long-sword still sheathed in its holster. The bike was heavily warded against any who might attempt to tamper with it, so he hadn't been worried. Still, it was *his* Harley and he'd have been pissed if it *had* been tampered with.

Zin's lust for blood was so fierce he could barely rein back the beast that threatened to take control and explode from within him. Gone was his desire to play with his food. He simply wanted to feed, regain his strength, and return to Hannah.

It was Hannah he wanted to be with, Hannah he wanted to share blood with.

He slipped into the shadows, waiting for his meal. This time two women strode out of the nightclub, heading toward him. Zin called to them with his mind, trapped them with his powers. Their blood sang to him, throbbing so loud it filled his senses. He backed the women against the wall where they waited calmly for him, as if their will was his. Usually he would have been intrigued by this lovely pair before him, but he felt no lust for these women, other than for their blood.

He was so weak from the *Lopos* poison, and so intent on his desire to feed, that he almost didn't see the dark shadow flying toward him.

At the last second, Zin dodged the poison-tipped spear aimed at his throat. The *Lopos* shrieked as Zin wheeled around and swung out one leg, catching the hideous creature off-balance. Spear still in hand, the beast shot to its feet and straight toward Zin.

At the same time another *Lopos* came from the shadows— only its target was the women quietly standing in the shadows next to the wall.

With a furious growl, Zin unsheathed the dagger strapped to his side. He dropped and rolled, avoiding the first beast. The creature slammed into the wall. The building shook, and smashed adobe rained down on him. The beast's spear skittered across the empty lot.

Zin rolled to his feet with amazing grace and agility and caught the second *Lopos* in the belly with his dagger. The beast screamed its rage as black poison spurted out of the rent. With a quick movement, Zin slit the beast's throat, unfortunately not enough to behead it—only enough to stop the creature's attack and send it fleeing into the night.

Damn, but he needed to get to his sword. No time. No time! The other *Lopos* was charging toward the women. The creature's eyes gleamed red, its sharp-toothed maw wide as its claws stretched out, aimed at their hearts.

Zin's head spun from the poison, but he had to save the innocents. He flung himself into the beast, slamming it into the ground. The rotted-meat stench of the creature nearly overwhelmed him.

The *Lopos* slashed its razor-like nails across Zin's throat.

Pain ripped through Zin as the claw marks burned with *Lopos* poison.

Zin rammed his dagger into the beast's chest.

It howled with fury, but still reached his claws toward Zin's chest, intending to take his heart.

With his last remaining strength Zin used his mental powers to call to Creed at the same time he jerked up on the dagger. He split breastbone as the dagger tore up the beast's chest, its throat, and then cleaved the *Lopos'* skull in two.

The beast collapsed to the ground, its howl of agony searing the night, and then its cry blew away in a swirl on the wind.

Zin dropped his head back, overwhelmed by agony and excruciating pain. New poison joined with old, turning his body into a well of misery. He couldn't move, could barely keep his eyes open. Finally he gave himself up to the darkness, all thought and feeling scattering with a last shuddering breath.

* * * * *

Hannah woke to the sound of rain hammering the house and a male voice rumbling in the distance. She had the feeling something wasn't quite right.

Monsoon, her sleepy brain informed her, even as she imagined sheets of water washing the desert clean all around them. The energy of the desert monsoon felt contagious—almost overpowering—as she eased up in the bed, pushed her dark hair out of her face, and glanced sleepily around the room.

Still Zin's room. Still Zin's bed.

Warmth rushed through her at the thought of really sharing the bed with Zin. The man turned her on in ways no other ever had. Her belly fluttered at just the mere idea of enjoying sex with Mr. Tall, Dark and Vampire, but then she shook her head at the train of her thoughts.

I have the hots for a vampire. She rolled her eyes and stared up at the dark ceiling. "Life can't get much more interesting, can it?"

The rain came harder and the male voice grew louder. Hannah slipped out of the bed, still clad only in Zin's black T-shirt.

Monsoon winds lashed rain against the shuttered windows, and candles flickered and spat in multiple sconces on the walls. A quick swirl of chill air whirled around her feet, as if coming from a door that had been opened, then shut again.

She padded across the room over smooth tiles, through the doorway and down the hall to the great room, where she came up short.

Shadows danced over Zin, who was stretched out on the bare floor, a gaping wound at his throat.

Hannah's hand flew to her mouth as she stared in horror at the body of the man who had been so vital, so alive when she saw him last.

Was he dead?

A tall golden-haired man in a long black coat stood over Zin's body. "Where do you want him, Patricia?"

"*Dios mio*, Creed." Concern etched Patricia's features as she waved him in the direction Hannah was standing. "To his room."

Hannah's heart pounded and cold fear rushed her as the blond man strode past her without even acknowledging her presence. She followed him into the room where he lowered Zin to the turquoise bed sheet, the same sheet she'd been lying on just moments before.

"Is he…" Her voice sounded hollow and small in the large room as she came up behind the man. "Is he…" she started again but stopped, unable to ask the question.

The man Patricia had called Creed turned his golden gaze on Hannah and she caught her breath. Those eyes captured her, eyes that held centuries of wisdom and pain. Eyes that frightened and consoled her all at once.

"He'll live." Creed seemed to dismiss her presence as he turned his back to her and placed his hand above the gaping wound at Zin's neck. "For now, at least. Long enough for us to help."

Hannah inched closer, and her fingers crept to her own throat as she watched. It was almost as if she could feel his pain, could feel the blood flowing from her in the same way it was oozing from Zin. She glanced up at Creed whose eyes were closed. His lips moved and he muttered words she couldn't understand.

Her gaze returned to Zin and she gave a soft gasp. While she watched, the wound seemed to knit itself shut. Slowly, starting at one side and working its way to the other, the wound closed until only a jagged purple line remained.

Patricia bustled in with a crystal glass of thick red fluid, and Hannah bit her lower lip and grimaced.

"That will not be enough to heal him." Creed motioned to Hannah and she gave a start of surprise. "He needs what only you can offer him."

Hannah's eyes widened and fear caused her heart to pound even faster.

"Why not me, Creed?" Patricia set the glass of her concoction on the end table. "I'm willing, and my blood is healthy. The girl is frightened. Don't push her, okay?"

His eyes met Patricia's. "The strength of your heart would aid him, but he needs her power. The power of their union."

Hannah's head buzzed. Without consciously realizing what she was doing, her feet carried her closer to the bed, and with every step, her fear mounted. Fear for Zin and whatever it was that caused him to look so deathly ill.

And fear for whatever it was that Creed wanted her to give.

When she reached Zin's side, Creed grabbed her wrist in a movement so fast that she reflexively tried to step back. But he held her firm in his grip. "Zin needs your blood." Creed's golden eyes were fierce and unwavering. "You have the choice of aiding him or refusing him."

Swallowing back the fear rising up in her throat, Hannah whispered, "And if I refuse?"

"He will die from *Lopos* poisoning." Creed's features hardened and his fangs gleamed in the dim lighting. It didn't even surprise her that he was a vampire, too. "In great quantities, the poison is the only thing that can kill a vampire other than the removal of his heart or his head."

"And...my blood is all he needs?"

Creed gave a slow nod. "I made sure Zin had a draught of fresh human blood before I brought him here, but yes, he needs yours more than any. You have power, both as his destined Eternal Mate, and all on your own. I don't understand it, but I've seen it." His voice grew more solemn as he added, "I can't— won't—force you, but if you refuse Zin, he'll die."

Patricia looked stricken.

She didn't know about the Eternal Mate nonsense, yet Hannah understood the dire need Zin had at this moment. The thought of him dying felt wrong in the universe, wrong in the grand scheme of rights and wrongs. More than that, the thought of his death felt like a weight crushing Hannah's soul. Even if he hadn't saved her life the night before by sucking the *Lopos* poison from her body, she knew she had to help save him, whatever the price. Letting her wrist relax in Creed's grip, she said, "Tell me what I need to do."

Patricia mumbled a quick prayer of thanks. "You won't be sorry. You won't be. If he ever makes you sorry, I'll tear out his heart myself, okay?"

Hannah managed a wry smile. "I'll remember that."

And then all other sensations faded, except Creed's grip on her wrist.

What am I doing? Oh, god. What's about to happen to me?

As if in answer, the monsoon howled and once more doubled its force. Wind and rain seemed to rattle the house on its foundation.

Creed broke his forceful stare and turned her wrist so that the soft underside was exposed. One vein stood out, dark and throbbing against her pale skin, as if waiting for this moment. It actually ached, that vein, like it was too full, like it needed draining.

Growling, Creed bent and sniffed the spot where the vein touched her flesh. "Healthy," he murmured in a scary, hungry way. "Unpolluted."

His fangs seemed to grow to the floor. They were so long! A little curved. And the way they gleamed in the low light reminded Hannah of prehistoric beasts. She clenched her teeth as she waited for Creed to use those horrifying fangs to tear into her wrist. Instead, he straightened, withdrew a dagger from inside his long black coat, and in an instant, sliced open her vein. Hannah cried out at the sharp, immediate pain.

"*Dios*," Patricia whispered. "Be careful, Creed."

But even as she spoke, Creed pulled Hannah's bleeding wrist down to Zin's mouth. He pressed the burning skin against Zin's lips, and immediately, they parted. Hannah gasped as she felt the coolness of his mouth, and the way her blood seemed to rush out of her body and into his.

For a long moment, she felt dizzy, like she might faint. Hannah blinked furiously, cheeks suddenly burning from the reaction of her body. Her nipples hardened. Her clit swelled and started to ache. She wanted to throw herself on Zin, demand that he wake, and force him to satisfy her. It took seconds. Just seconds!

"Steady," Creed instructed.

Hannah didn't look at him, or at Patricia. She felt like her rabid desire was written in scarlet letters across her face. She watched Zin feeding from her even as his eyes remained closed.

"Will I turn into a vampire?" She couldn't help the edge of fear and embarrassment in her voice.

Creed gave a soft laugh. "Not from this, little one. Only from a vampire bite, and only if the vampire takes too much blood. The *Vampiros* are always careful not to turn a human who doesn't wish to be turned. Renegade vampires are not so charitable."

Hannah nodded as Creed pressed her wrist tighter to Zin's mouth. He began to suck hard, a low growl rising up in his throat.

Burning pain flowed through Hannah's body, and her head began to feel lighter still. But she didn't want to pull away. Not yet. Not until she was sure Zin was going to be all right. Before her eyes, his color seemed to be improving. His wounded body seemed to be mending itself. Even the jagged purple line across his neck became fainter as he sucked blood from her wrist.

At the same time, despite the pain, Hannah's desire doubled. It tripled. She started to sway and shake. Any minute, she'd have an orgasm with these two strangers watching, and then she'd die of humiliation. For all of her bravado, Hannah really didn't want an audience for such intimate occurrences. A fan section of one would do splendidly, in fact.

A tingle started between her legs, traveling up and out like a sharp electric wave.

I can't be coming. Please, don't let me come.

At the same time, if she didn't get relief, she might combust on the spot.

Zin drew more of her essence into his mouth. Hannah felt the most exquisite sensation each time he swallowed, and wondered distantly if men felt like this when they came inside a woman they loved. Her fluids were filling him, bringing life. It was wild. And she was a second from the most intense orgasm she had ever felt. One more suck, one more swallow…

"Enough." Creed pulled her away from Zin's blood-smeared lips.

Hannah actually cried out in shock and frustration, but Creed ignored her. He held his hand over her wrist, and at once the blood stopped flowing.

It took a few seconds, but Hannah's arousal slowly lessened. Sanity reasserted itself, and she found she couldn't take her eyes off Zin. He seemed to have fallen into a peaceful sleep.

"Is he going to be okay now?" she whispered, vaguely aware that the storm was waning outside. She felt herself fade dizzily with it, weaving in and out of awareness.

"Yes," came Creed's curt answer.

"Here, baby." Patricia wiped the remaining blood from Hannah's wrist with a soft damp towel. "Come with me. You'll need food and rest now."

"Whoa." Hannah's head spun and she felt the absurd desire to giggle. "Rest first."

Without waiting for either of them to respond, and barely conscious of what she was doing, she slid onto the bed and curled up beside Zin.

Chapter Seven
Early Afternoon

Something warm and soft stirred beside Zin and he slowly opened his eyes. Hannah was snuggled up to him, her back to his chest, her bottom snug against his cock.

His very erect cock. It was a wonder he could breathe as tight as it was against his leather pants. Just the merest movement and he could surely climax.

Hannah murmured something in her sleep and snuggled closer to him. Zin let out a soft groan. She was going to kill him.

He raised himself up on his elbow and watched Hannah as she slept. Her hair was tousled, her eyelashes dark crescents against her tanned skin. Her breathing was slow and steady, and she cradled one arm to her chest. Carefully he reached his arm over her and slipped his fingers around her hand. With a feather light touch he brushed his thumb over the purple slit across her wrist. She'd given him her blood last night to save him. And she'd done it of her own free will. Creed never would have forced her, and Patricia would have killed him if he'd tried.

Even though he'd been barely conscious last night, he remembered Creed bearing him home. Remembered the sweet taste of Hannah's blood as it flowed over his tongue and through his body. Creed had been right. There was a strength and power within Hannah that had healed him faster than any other human blood could have.

She was still wearing his T-shirt, but it was hiked up so that her hip was bared to him. Her smooth, golden skin beckoned, and it was all he could do to hold himself back and not reach around her thigh, tangle his fingers in the dark curls of her mound, and slide into her wetness. He scented her nectar and it called to him as much as her blood did.

Blood that now flowed through his veins.

Hannah murmured and stirred again and Zin gently moved his fingers up her arm, down her side, to her bare hip. He caressed the perfect skin and groaned at the feel of her silky flesh beneath his palm. She was so, so warm. So alive. Her blood pulsed beneath his fingertips in a deep, throbbing tone.

Zin breathed in the scent of her, and it filled his senses like an aphrodisiac. He slid his hand down to her flat belly and pressed his cock tighter against the cleft of her ass. Almost without thought, he slowly pumped his hips against hers, making the ache in his cock even greater than before.

Hannah blinked away the last threads of sleepiness to find herself on fire. It took her a moment to realize that she was no longer in a dream world with her fantasy man...that she was actually in bed with him.

His hand burned her belly, and his cock was hard against her backside. His unique scent surrounded her, making her nipples rise and her pussy grow instantly damp. He nuzzled her hair, murmuring soft words in an ancient language, and slowly moved his mouth to her neck where he nipped at her skin.

With a soft moan, Hannah arched into his touch at the same time she brought her hand to his. She moved his hand to her breast and gasped when he pinched her nipple. Pleasure coursed her body.

Don't start this, her mind warned. *You never get to finish.*

But she couldn't help herself. She held Zin's hand in place, glorying in the way his fingers felt on her aching nipple.

He pinched and tweaked, giving pressure then letting go, until her body jerked from the rhythm — and he stopped. Started over. *Took over.*

Hannah felt the shift in subtle waves of want, knowing Zin was now in control, realizing her needs were betraying her. She wasn't sure she cared.

Then, before she knew what was happening, she was suddenly flat on her back and Zin was between her thighs, his arms braced to either side of her head. He pressed his hips to hers, his cock hard against her pussy even through his leather pants. He looked dark and sexy, his black eyes alight with a fiery need.

Just like he had in her dreams. So many times.

"Good morning, *mi alma*," he said with a smile so carnal it made her bite her own lip.

"Morning." She glanced at his neck, where the purple line of his wound was now so faint she could barely see it. "Um, you're all better now?"

"Mmmm." He lowered his head and kissed her temple. "You're still weak. You need to eat."

Food was the last thing on Hannah's mind at that moment, but Zin rolled away from her.

See? her mind chattered. *I told you so. You always starve to death at this banquet, damn it.*

Hannah closed her eyes until she could manage her desire. When she opened them again, Zin was standing beside the bed. He held out his hand and she took it. Her body burned for him, and she knew he wanted her just as much. Still, he concentrated on her well-being, on what was best for her in that moment. Food, human food, to restore her strength.

She wondered at this man, who could have taken her any time, by force or with her begging—but he didn't. He was waiting for something, but...what?

She let him lead her toward the kitchen and her stomach growled at the delicious smells coming from the door. Patricia smiled at them both and waved Hannah to a seat at the table.

With a nod to Patricia, Zin said, "I'll be in my study."

"Do you have to go?" Hannah asked, sad beyond reason, her eyes not wanting to leave his face.

"Yes, he does." Patricia's firm answer settled the issue. "The man is a walking distraction. Besides, he's my blackmail. You don't get him again until you've eaten all of this. Understand?"

Hannah barely held back a groan, but she nodded.

Zin had no need for sustenance having been replenished with Hannah's blood, so he turned away from the breakfast.

He felt restless, edgy, and in the need of some good ol' rock-n-roll.

His study was actually a small soundstage and recording studio, all created to indulge his hobby. Carefully, he shut the soundproof door behind him. He retrieved his electric guitar, turned on the amps and tuned the instrument. When he was satisfied, he laid into an old song by the band Led Zeppelin, *Highway to Heaven*. He belted out the tune, playing with ferocious intensity, wondering if Hannah would take him to Heaven tonight.

If Hannah had her choice, no doubt she'd push him away with everything she had.

But he didn't plan to let her off that easy.

When the last strains of the last chord died away, the sound of a person clapping jerked his attention toward the doorway. Hannah stood there, a surprised smile on her face. How had she managed to slip into his sanctuary without him being aware of her?

As her clapping died away, she closed the door behind her and moved toward the small stage. "A vampire who rocks." She laughed, the sound itself music to his ears. "I never would have believed it. And you're good, too. Do you play professionally?"

He gave her an amused look. "Wouldn't fit into my tight schedule."

"Can you just see it now?" She picked up his acoustic guitar from where it rested against the wall and moved to one of the chairs by the stage. "Zin Plant, rock-n-roll legend."

Zin couldn't help but smile at her teasing way of relating him to the famous recording artist. To his surprise, she settled herself on one of the comfortable cushioned chairs and began to tune the guitar. "You play?"

She made a face at him. "No, I just tune guitars for fun."

He folded his arms across his chest and watched her. "Now who's being sarcastic?"

Hannah just smiled, and suddenly he realized she was completely at ease, as if this was her element. And when she began to play the acoustic guitar he could tell that it was. He'd been playing for at least a hundred years, but what came out of his instrument under her hand was pure magic.

"I leave now to go to Laredo, my love, I come here to say farewell.

While I'm there I will sorely miss you, my love, how much I can never tell.

And this golden key, now take it, my love, and open my secret heart;

How much I shall always want you, my love and how great my pain to part."

Laredo. *Gods. Why that song?*

When she sang, he thought he'd die on the spot. Her voice was truly that of an angel, her song the light to his dark, as was her soul.

When the last note died away, she dampened the strings and her golden-green eyes met his. "Nice guitar."

"I've heard you before." Not that particular song, but her voice. "I should have realized it, but I was too caught up in you."

Hannah's eyes widened at that simple statement. The words made a low thrill swirl in her belly.

I was too caught up in you.

His black gaze focused on her and she shrugged. "It's a living."

He shook his head, his long black hair brushing his shoulders. "You live for what you do. You live to sing and perform. There's been nothing else for you."

She couldn't take his intense scrutiny any longer and she turned back to the guitar and this time picked out the melody that had come to her as she drove toward Cabo, before stopping at the hotel.

"What about you?" she asked as she softly played the guitar. "Being a vampire and all."

"It's a living." He sat on the chair next to her. "Will you...sing with me?" The urge was unbearable to Zin. He knew he had to hear her again. He'd sing anything she wanted, so long as they could harmonize, so long as he could hear the sweet sound of her voice filling the air.

Hannah gave him a sexy smile, then fired up *Laredo* one more time.

Zin's chest tightened as he sang the words with her, actually stumbling in the second verse when they reached the toughest line.

It holds all my great devotion, my love, my passion and sometimes my pain...

Yes, yes. That's what her voice did to him. It was the golden key to the chest of treasures in his soul. And that fast, Hannah had opened the chest. If she looked, she could see his devotion, his love, his passion, his pain.

But would she look?

Zin barely managed to hold his own and finish the song.

After a few minutes of silence, Hannah asked her question again. "What's it like, being a vampire?"

"I told you—it's a living." Zin was surprised he could speak at all.

Hannah shot a glance at him to see his teasing smile, but then her expression became unsettled. "Do you...do you kill the people you take blood from?"

With a slow shake of his head he said, "Never. I take only enough, only what I need. I don't harm them in any way, and I repay humanity with my protection, whenever the chance arises."

Hannah nodded but frowned and continued to pick the eerie melody from the guitar. "So, do you turn people into vampires, often?"

"I never take enough blood to start the transformation." He shrugged. "If the process starts, you have to finish it. Otherwise, the person stays trapped between being a vampire and being human. They have blood-thirst, but none of the powers or the immortality that Vampires have. It's a horrible fate."

For a moment she looked lost in thought as the strummed the guitar. "How long have you been a vampire?" she finally asked.

His voice was quiet as he said, "Over 500 years."

Hannah abruptly stopped playing. "You're joking."

It was his turn to shrug. "I was an Aztec warrior before I was made."

She could see it then. In his fierce black eyes, his features, his regal bearing.

The next question that came to her mind surprised her, but then, considering what she'd been through, along with her nightmares, perhaps it wasn't such an unexpected question. "The Aztec sacrifices...were you a part of them?"

Zin's expression hardened. For a long minute—far, far too long—he didn't answer. When he did, his voice was hoarse with rage. "It's far more complicated than that. The beasts, the *Lopos*, they once set themselves up as the gods of the ancients."

Hannah's brows narrowed in concentration.

"You met only two of the so-called 'gods,' Huitzilopochtli and his mother, Coatlicue. In truth, they were ravening monsters who preyed upon my people. They demanded blood of the weak and hearts of the strong, or else they terrorized our city."

He scowled and she could see the anger, frustration, and pain in his expression. "I grew up knowing this, but still I hated it. Most of our people felt the same way, and lived in fear of who was to be the next sacrifice. We were powerless. I lost friends, family…"

He clenched his fists so hard his knuckles turned white. "As a *Mexica* warrior I helped to capture warriors of other nations to be sacrificed to appease the *Lopos*, rather than those of our own blood. I had no choice. It was my duty to save my own people." He swallowed then added in a husky timber as his gaze met hers, "But for one I was too late…"

Zin's pain drew Hannah to him. She set the guitar aside. Leaning it against a chair, she moved to kneel next to him. She slipped between his thighs, wrapped her arms around his waist, and settled her face against his chest. The beat of his heart was strong and fierce beneath her ear and his bearing was stiff from remembered pains. He smelled of leather and night sky, and felt so right within her arms.

Gradually he relaxed in her grasp and stroked her hair. "These are old wounds, *mi alma*. Do not trouble yourself with them."

So many questions rose in her mind. She wanted to learn everything she could about him. He intrigued her in ways no man had ever before, but then she'd never met a vampire, either.

"You have a heartbeat." She tilted her head to look up at him. "I thought vampires didn't have hearts or souls."

A mischievous glint sparked in his black eyes. "And garlic and crosses scare us shitless."

She wrinkled her nose. "All right then, Mr. Bad Boy Vampire. What is real?"

"We have hearts and souls." He cupped her chin, his calloused fingers rough against her skin. "Patricia keeps crucifixes all over this place, and sometimes she puts garlic in those terrible drinks she makes."

Hannah had to laugh. She could picture the housekeeper doing just that. "No coffin either, eh?"

"Nope." His mouth twisted into an amused grin. "A stake in the heart or beheading—now that would hurt."

She gave him a thoughtful look. "So what other vampire myths are actually true?"

"We are immortal." Zin stroked his thumb along her jaw line. "Sunlight will fry us and we're very sensitive to any kind of light." He gave her a teasing grin. "Especially whatever freaky ass shit you do when you glow."

"Oops." She did her best to look as innocent as possible. "And you can really fly…that's just so unreal."

"You ought to try it sometime." His fingers lightly stroked her earlobe. "You'd make a beautiful vampiress."

"Not going there." She shook her head, freeing herself from his sensual touch. "You can read minds, I know. What else?"

He shrugged. "Shapeshifting. Every vampire has one form he can shift into."

Hannah frowned in concentration. "Yours is a jaguar?"

"Yes." His look was one of surprise. "How did you know?"

"I had the strangest dream…" She took a deep breath and changed the subject. "What about those *Lopos*—how did we get from *Mexica* warriors to what's happening now?"

With a sigh he said, "These are old wars we still fight today."

She studied his proud features, not liking the image of him fighting those hideous beasts who had tried to imprison her—probably even sacrifice her. "Do you fight them alone?"

He brushed his knuckles across her cheek, a feathery touch that made her melt against him. "Together the *Vampiros* battle the *Lopos*. We'll fight them until their deaths—or ours."

Hannah frowned. The thought of Zin dying tore at her heart and soul, even though she barely knew the man—the vampire—at all.

Instinctively she raised herself up on her knees, wanting to comfort him. She moved her hands from his waist, up his chest and then linked her fingers behind his neck. He looked down at her and she could see the centuries in his eyes, could feel the strength in his very being. That strength drew her, brought her into the circle of his embrace. He wrapped his arms around her, as if afraid he would lose her if he let go.

But still he waited, looking at her as if he were starving for his next meal. A man hungry for a woman, perhaps even for love. But after what she'd been through she worried she couldn't give him love, but she shared his hunger for greater intimacy.

Hannah tipped her face to his and kissed the corner of his mouth. His warm breath brushed her lips and she heard herself moan. But still he waited. She kissed his forehead, his cheek, the line of his jaw, and he held her tighter to him. Both had their eyes open as her lips met his in a soft brush.

"My heart knows you," he murmured, his mouth a mere breath apart from hers. "I've always known you."

Chapter Eight
Mid-afternoon

Hunger for his woman seized Zin with the force of a thousand warriors. His large hands spanned Hannah's small waist and he easily brought her onto his lap. She straddled him, smiling. Her arms were still around his neck, but now she was above him, her hair a dark fall over one shoulder.

She bent and nuzzled his hair and he heard her deep intake of breath, as if she were scenting him for the first time, imprinting his smell in her memory. "I don't understand it, but this feels so right." She kissed the tip of his ear. "*You* feel so right."

"I'll always be with you." Zin brushed his lips along the curve of her neck. Lust raged within him for her body, for her blood, and especially for her heart and soul. "I'll never let you go, Hannah. I won't lose you again."

"Don't push it, *mi Vampiro*." She paused and raised her head, golden-green eyes serious yet hungry. "For this moment, in this place and time, I want you, Zin."

Zin groaned. He battled the desire to ravage her, to take her like a predator. His fangs burst into his mouth, and it was all he could do not to slide them into the sweet flesh of her neck, to take the precious blood flowing through her veins.

While he held her with one hand he slipped his other into her hair and brought her head down so that he could kiss her with all the passion raging inside him. Yet still he held himself back, not wanting to hurt her, not wanting to frighten her with the beast that fought to free itself, fought to overtake him.

Hannah matched him with her fervor, kissing him with such intensity that his mind and his cock threatened to explode.

He could feel the mysterious power of light in her soul, the light threatening to break free and challenge the beast in his nature, yet she held it in check just as he reined in his darkness.

Their tongues mated, thrusting deep and pulling back, then thrusting again. Zin wanted to be together as completely as possible, to share everything with this woman. She ran her tongue along the serrated edge of his teeth and didn't even pause when she licked at his incisors. Instead she shuddered, as if in pleasure, and moaned into his mouth.

He nipped at her lower lip, a soft gentle bite, and she tangled her fingers in his hair, drawing him harder and tighter to her. When he broke the kiss her breasts were rising and falling beneath the black shirt she had borrowed from him and her nipples poked against the soft fabric.

"Don't make me wait any longer." She reached between them and caressed the outline of his steel-hard erection. "I feel like I've waited for years."

"I've waited centuries for you." He dipped his head and licked at one of her nipples, soaking the fabric. "I want our first time to be one we cherish for the centuries to come."

Hannah didn't argue with Zin's statement, even though she knew he would long outlive her. She was mortal and he was an immortal. Besides, she had a life away from his, and she'd have to go back to it soon.

But she wasn't going to think about any of that now. She *couldn't* think about it.

At this moment she just wanted this man, this vampire, more than she'd ever wanted a man in her life. Need roared through her like a fire gone wild, burning and burning as if it might turn her to cinders. That raw sense of power she'd been feeling mixed with her desire for Zin, and she had to fight to temper it, to keep the power, the light, at bay.

He cupped her naked buttocks beneath the T-shirt and kneaded her ass cheeks. Damn, but his hands were masterful. So powerful, yet gentle. With each squeeze, he seemed to claim her all over again, pulling her against his erection as he kissed her mouth, her neck, and each nipple in turn. One to the other and back again, wetting the fabric, making it cling, rubbing it hard against the throbbing nubs with his tongue.

She thought she could feel the tip of his sharp teeth against the cloth, nearly spearing through to the tips of her breasts. A fine, fine edge. Pleasure, waiting to be pain. The thought made her heart pound, turned her pussy to hot, wet, aching need.

Could she want him more? How was that possible?

"Zin, please!" She squeezed his cock, hard, and it jerked beneath the soft leather of his pants. "I can't wait any longer."

With a groan Zin raised his head, half-crazed with Hannah's scent, with the feel of her aroused body in his embrace. He kissed her as she continued to squeeze and rub the length of his erection. If he didn't watch it, he was going to come in his pants—something that hadn't happened to him since he was a youth, long before he was made.

Holding her tight to him, Zin rose from the chair, knelt, and settled Hannah back on the thick carpeting. The shirt she was wearing bunched around her hips, exposing her pussy. Her black curls were wet with her dew and her folds were already swollen with need.

"I could look at you for hours," he said truthfully. "And fuck you for endless hours more. Is that what you want?"

Hannah trembled at his words, in a moment so feminine, so vulnerable, he wanted to roar.

"Yes. Yes. Wait! Can vampires get women pregnant?"

Zin shook his head. "Nope. Comes with the territory. Can't catch or transmit any diseases either. I won't let anything happen to you, *mi alma*. I swear on my fangs, my heart's blood, and the noble history of my people."

Hannah hesitated, but quickly melted under Zin's hungry, smoldering gaze. After all, he had as much to lose as she did, right? If he didn't kill her—which she felt sure he wouldn't—she could expose him to the world, feed him to his enemies if he betrayed her.

Betrayal just didn't feel like an issue with Zin. Maybe it was all they'd been through already. Maybe it was because of the feeling that she'd had since meeting him — that she'd known him for centuries. She hadn't thought she could trust a man again, but Zin was different. With a new flood of warmth, she realized that the impossibilities she'd faced across the last two days had stripped away her past like a dead layer of skin. She had only her instincts now, and she had to honor them.

Her instincts…and her growing animal lust.

She smiled and raised her hips. "Well, what are you waiting for?"

Zin settled on his hands and knees between her thighs, and his eyes met hers. "I want to explore you, taste you, know all of you."

Hannah parted her lips to argue, but he rose up and kissed her firmly, stopping her from speaking at all. God, the way this man could kiss. He was making love to her with his mouth in the way she wanted his body to make love to her. Heat spread from her lips, down her neck, to her breasts and belly, and lower, making her pussy even wetter. She couldn't stand much more arousal. She'd scream if he didn't satisfy her soon.

When he drew away from the kiss, his eyes focused on hers. Gently he pushed her shirt up her body, kissing her belly as he eased the fabric up. He paused at the jaguar-etched ring at her navel, flicking his tongue around it and dipping into her belly button.

With a groan, Hannah felt the ring's electric pulls and tingles as Zin used it expertly. He moved it with his tongue, mimicking what she hoped he would do to her clit — and soon. She gripped his hair fiercely, to let him know she'd pull the strands straight out of his head if he tortured her much longer.

Rumbling with approval, he moved back up, pushing the T-shirt up and over her breasts. Nipping, kissing, tugging gently with his fearsome fangs, he made her feel like she had rings in both nipples, to be pulled and tugged at his whim. Her breasts were on fire as he sucked and bit, almost to the point of blood, almost to the point of exquisite agony—but not quite. Hannah was close to pounding on his head, but she couldn't stop running her fingers through the silk of his thick hair.

Zin's mouth plowed ahead like a pleasure machine, teasing and tantalizing each inch of her flesh until he reached the hollow of her throat. He scraped the sensitive skin with his teeth.

Hannah froze, no longer able to draw a full breath. The veins in her throat ached, they actually ached, and her head spun with images of him sinking those fangs inches deep into the well of her blood.

Fear competed with the new, odd desires. "No," she whimpered. "Not that. Not yet."

Zin growled, a low, fearsome sound that reminded her of the jaguar from her dream. For a moment, she sensed another aspect of his nature, feral and murderous and impossibly strong. And then it was gone, caged by her simple refusal.

I can trust him...I can...

In a quick movement Zin slid the T-shirt the rest of the way off, over her head and arms, then tossed it away so that she was completely naked beneath him. His vest was open, revealing his sculpted muscles, and the leather brushed her nipples, causing her to gasp at the incredible sensation. His leather-clad hips were between hers and he rubbed his erection in a slow erotic movement against her pussy.

"You are the most exquisite creature I have ever known." He braced himself over her and his black gaze wouldn't let her go.

She laced her fingers behind his neck. "Don't make me wait anymore, Zin."

"*Mi alma*, I have waited so long for you." The fierce intensity and emotion in his gaze nearly brought tears to her eyes.

He lowered his head and kissed her cheek. She gave a soft moan as his erection brushed her belly. This time, when his fangs scraped her neck she didn't pull away. This man wouldn't take more than she was willing to give.

Slowly his mouth devoured her without drawing the slightest drop of blood. Kissing her collarbone, the hollow of her throat, pausing to return to the curve of her neck. She could sense his lust. It teemed in his eyes each time he gazed at her. She could hear it in the ragged catch of his breathing. Zin wanted even more from her, emotions and commitments far beyond flesh or even blood.

That was way more than she was prepared to deal with. No matter what he thought, there couldn't be a future between them. There could only be here and now.

And here and now would be wonderful.

He swept his mouth away from her neck and moved to the sensitive spot between her breasts. A groan rolled out of him as he moved his lips to one of her nipples and lightly flicked it with his tongue, causing Hannah to arch up to meet him.

"Zin, please." She knew she was begging, but the man was tormenting her, driving her mad beyond all reason. Her pussy was so wet she felt her juices sliding down her thighs. "God, that feels so good. So, so good. Please fuck me."

But he ignored her, taking his time to lick and suck each of her nipples. She cupped her breasts, lifting them up high and pressing them together so that he could easily brush his mouth from one peak to the other. Hannah raised her head and flicked her tongue alongside his against her nipple and his fangs. In tandem, they moved to her other nipple, both of them licking and sucking. Hannah caught his lip again and again, and traced the white hardness of the teeth she should be terrified to see.

She wasn't.

Something about those fangs, poised just above her nipples, biting down on the darkened tips, nearly made her come from sheer excitement.

Hannah moaned as he moved away and trailed his lips along the line down the center of her abs.

"Keep playing with your nipples," he ordered as he continued lower, and lower. "And keep your eyes on me. Watch what I do to you."

Hannah was way past debating. She pinched and pulled at her wet nubs and held them up high enough that she could flick her tongue over them while he gazed at her. By his pained expression she knew it turned him on. She deliberately gave long slow licks from one nipple to the next as he slowly kissed his way down to her pussy.

Hannah arched her hips as Zin nuzzled the dark curls of her mound. "What would you like me to do, *mi alma?*"

She pinched her nipples hard and raised her hips higher, toward his face. "Taste me. All of me. Lick my clit."

"I've wanted to taste you from the first moment I held you in my arms." His smile was something beyond hungry. "From the moment I scented you."

Zin slipped his finger into her wet channel, and Hannah felt the most delicious, soul-gripping shock. Connection. Something deeper.

Yes...

She gave a little scream of frustration as he pulled the finger back out. Instantly, he teased her clit with his thumb, then thrust his finger back inside her wet walls, in and out, in and out. Sweat beaded on her skin. The world narrowed to the room, the patch of rug where they lay, the length and width of the finger driving her closer and closer to the edge of insanity. She could barely breathe. She was so close to coming, and he'd barely begun to touch her where she needed him most.

"The scent of your woman's musk—there's nothing better. It fills my senses." He lowered his face and breathed deeply, as if drawing her essence into him to keep forever. Then he flicked his tongue along her folds and Hannah cried out from the sensation. Sizzling perfection, just the right pressure.

"You taste as sweet as your scent, *mi corazón*."

Hannah squirmed at the exquisite feel of his tongue lapping at her clit and the slight brush of his fangs against her swollen folds. She no longer feared him for what he was. Rather it excited her, made her want to know everything about him. She definitely wasn't ready for him to take her blood, but she wanted his cock planted firmly inside her. "Zin...*please*."

But he seemed intent on driving her to distraction. She moved her hands from her breasts and gripped his long hair in her hands. She pressed her pussy tighter to his face and he growled a primal sound of satisfaction and need.

God, she felt her climax building and building and then she felt Zin *touch* her mind, felt his presence everywhere—outside and in. His hands slid beneath her ass and he raised her up, feeding off her juices, feeding off her lust for him.

He paused and looked at her, his mouth wet with her essence. "Play with your nipples again. Watch me while I watch you."

Hannah groaned with the need to come. "Stop teasing me."

"Do what I say, Hannah."

She obeyed, not wanting him to drive her even crazier than he already was.

"Good." He smiled and watched her as she brought her hands to her breasts. "Keep watching me, or I'll stop. Understand?"

"Hurry," she demanded. "I can't take much more."

He gave a soft laugh and lowered his mouth to her folds, but kept his eyes on hers. Hannah pinched and pulled at her nipples as she watched him licking her pussy. Her eyelids threatened to lower, but he paused and she screamed her frustration again—this time louder. She bit her lower lip and pinched her nipples harder as he plunged two fingers into her channel and licked her clit. He drove her hard then pulled back, brought her to the brink again, then backed off.

Tears streamed down Hannah's cheeks. "Please, Zin. I'm begging you."

He gave her a devilish smile, then sucked on her clit so hard that she came at once. Her orgasm burst through her entire being and her body flared with a brief burst of blue-white light as she lost control. She cried out, long and hard, the light filling her mind and her senses—incredible, endless, throbbing—she'd never felt anything like it, and it seemed to last forever.

When she came down from her high, she saw the glow had faded from her skin. Zin was kissing the inside of her thigh, his eyes closed, and she trembled with another aftershock just from the feel of his lips pressed against her soft flesh.

"Are you finished trying to blind me?" he asked in a teasing tone as he opened his eyes and looked at her.

"I think so." Her voice quavered and she reached out her arms for him but he drew away. "Although you might want to wear sunglasses if I have another orgasm like that one."

"I'll keep that in mind." Zin's expression grew more intense as he rose up on his knees and slipped off his vest, giving her a full view of his impressive chest and biceps. "I have a feeling I'm going to need the darkest ones I can find."

"Just shut up and fuck me." She squirmed and hooked her legs around his waist so that he was forced closer to her. "I want that cock right where it belongs."

"And where is that?" He unfastened his leather pants and pushed them down far enough to free his erection and his balls. *Da-amn.* The man *did* have a cock the size of a policeman's baton.

"I want you in my pussy." She rubbed her palms over her nipples and clamped her legs tighter around his waist as she watched him. "Right now."

"You're going to have to let me go so I can take off my pants and boots." He tried to free himself, but she shook her head and kept her legs firmly around him.

"No. I want you to fuck me just like you are. Now."

Zin gave her that sexy soul-searing grin and lowered himself so that his hands were braced to either side of her again. He lowered his head and kissed her hard, and she tasted herself upon his lips and tongue.

"What's the rush, *mi alma*?" He moved his mouth down her neck to one of her breasts and licked the nipple, flicking his tongue back and forth across the hard nub. "We have hours yet before I need to go out and hunt."

"*Hours?* Do you want a laser show on your hands?" She reached between them and stroked his cock and rubbed it against the folds of her pussy. "Because I'm ready to go nuclear on you."

Zin smiled down at his woman. Even with her fading scratches and bruises, she was so incredibly beautiful. Her dark hair was a black spray of silk against the taupe carpeting, her olive complexion and golden-green eyes a perfect compliment.

After five centuries he was finally going to join with the woman who'd captured his heart. The moment was so precious, so clear, that he was almost afraid that it would vanish in the blink of an eye.

But she remained beneath him, biting her lower lip and straining to get closer to him. She was real. This moment was real.

Slowly he allowed her to guide him into her pussy. She was slick and tight, and he groaned aloud at the feel of her channel gripping him, taking him deep. "You feel so perfect, *mi alma*," he murmured as he slowly moved inside her. "So very perfect. Like I've always dreamed you would be."

"Yes." Tears glistened on her eyelashes as he paused, pressed tight inside her, and she wrapped her arms around his neck.

Zin crushed his mouth to hers, just keeping his cock buried within her and not moving. He kissed her long and hard, then began moving in and out of her, fucking her with all his heart and soul. Her nipples rasped against his chest, and her thighs clenched tight around his hips.

Hannah felt like she was dying. Each time the man moved, small orgasms washed over her and a slight glow rolled over her skin as she fought to mute the light, to control it even as *she* lost control. Her pussy contracted again and again, gripping and releasing his cock. He felt like perfect, smooth wood, yet hot and flexible. The fullness took her breath away. She felt joined to him, vulnerable, yet stronger than ever. Hannah threw back her head and moaned.

Zin felt more contractions on his cock. He thrust into her harder and harder yet, and she cried out with another orgasm, this one so powerful and intense that Zin felt it to the soles of his boots. Her body flared, nearly blinding him, but he sensed her reining it in even as her body convulsed.

Lust for every part of his woman built like an oncoming monsoon. The beast in his *Vampiro* heart threatened to burst free, and if it did there would be no calling it back. He needed to taste her blood, needed that connection like he'd never needed it before.

But he would never betray her trust. Would not take blood from her until she offered herself to him.

He concentrated on driving her into one orgasm after another, on giving her pleasures only *Vampiros* knew how to give.

She moaned and thrashed, taking him deeper, holding him close, until he could wait no longer. With a warrior's cry, he climaxed, his hot semen flowing into her channel.

At that, Hannah gave her loudest shout yet, and came with him in a bone-jarring wave of trembling and shaking. He continued his thrusts until he climaxed a second time, bringing Hannah along with him again and yet again.

As he slowed his rhythm, he gazed down at her.

She had managed to restrain her power of light. Her eyes were closed. Her breathing was shallow, yet even.

He'd exhausted her.

Good. As it should be.

"*Mi alma*," he whispered, kissing her forehead.

For a time, he lay with his cock inside her, listening to the sweet sounds of her sleeping.

And then he slipped himself free and tucked his cock back into his pants. He sat up against the chair and pulled her into his lap.

Zin's senses hummed with alertness despite his need to sleep after such perfect sex.

He couldn't sleep. He wouldn't. He would do his duty this time, and guard this woman, his heart, the other part of his soul, with every ounce of energy, strength, and cunning he possessed — even if he never slept again.

"I won't fail you twice, my love." Zin pressed his lips against Hannah's hair. "Whatever it takes."

Chapter Nine
Morning

"Woman, don't make me apply the age-old code." Britt's voice had a sharp, but good-humored edge. "Thou shalt not abandon best girlfriends for anything with a cock, no matter how gorgeous, long, thick, or perfect that cock might be."

"I know, I know." Hannah laughed. It had been a whole week since she'd first come to Zin's house and Brit wasn't too happy about it. "But you've got phone numbers and the address now, and we'll do Cozumel next month, I swear."

"Keep your promises, Hannah," Britt intoned like a demented fortuneteller. "Else I'll come remove that perfect cock and store it in a jar!"

"Hey, I've written four new songs. Four! You know how blocked I was. It's great here—and you're nuts."

"Horny would be more accurate. But, since I don't have you to compete with, these beaches are *mine*."

Hannah could well imagine her friend in a barely-there thong bikini, making natives and tourists alike very, very restless. Britt's golden-brown skin and her tumbling black ringlets got her noticed wherever she went.

That's the thing about mixed-race parents, she was fond of quipping. *You get the best of both worlds, baby.*

"Listen, sweetie." Britt changed tones in a hurry. "A little bad news, but don't wig out on me."

"What?" Hannah instantly felt ice in her belly. She started to shiver. Was it her sister? God, no—her mother? The facility had Britt's number...

"That bastard, Tim the Dimdick. I think I saw him skulking around here. In fact, I'm pretty sure of it. No doubt he's trying to snap a picture or dig up some dirt—make a few more bucks at your expense."

Relief claimed Hannah for a minute, then anger replaced all other emotions. "If you see him again, shoot him."

Britt hesitated, as if seriously considering this option. "I wish they made dart guns with poison that would shrivel up balls. Since they don't, I'll leave him to the tender mercy of civil court when you sue him."

Hannah sighed. "I don't want to sue him. I just want to forget about him, and I want him to leave me alone."

"Best that you stay put wherever you are. I doubt old Tim Dimdick could find you there if he tried."

Forcing herself back to more pleasant thoughts, Hannah remembered what else she needed to ask. "A favor," she said in her best pretty-please voice. "I know I don't have much room to ask—but would you do something for me?"

"Anything. But hurry. The sun's up and the bronze gods await."

"Call my sister for me? You know how protective Nicki gets. She'll eat me alive if I try to explain all this."

Never mind the kidnapping and vampire aspects, which Hannah had deliberately kept to herself. No one needed Britt showing up in a tank mounted with spotlights and jammed with crosses, garlic, and wooden stakes.

"You don't want much do you?" A pause, and then, "Okay, but you owe me a new bathing suit. No, no. For Nicki, two new suits. Deal?"

"Thong or high-cut?" Hannah answered automatically.

"Thong, honey. I'm not old yet. Now, don't forget to call me at our appointed time. I'd hate to have to fly down there to Oz on my broom and tell that horny bastard to surrender my Dorothy."

After a throaty laugh that reminded Hannah of Britt's incredible talents as a singer in her own right, Britt hung up. No doubt already getting naked and reaching for her thong.

"Who am I kidding? She was naked when I called."

Hannah shook her head, glanced around the odd Ops room, then dialed the next number. The vampire spy center seemed cool and quiet compared to the rest of the house, and the ringing on the other end of the line sounded distant.

On the eighth ring, a false-happy voice said, "Desert Shadow Homes. May I help you?"

"I need to speak to Angel." Hannah gave the appropriate codes to identify herself, then waited for the companion nurse to come on the line.

As she waited she studied her forearm. The mark was completely gone from the night Creed had slit her wrist to feed Zin. Every wound she'd had on her body when she'd first met Zin had vanished, not a trace left.

"Hello, Miss Hannah," came the warm, welcome voice on the other end of the line. "Your mama, she's fine. Ate all her food yesterday, and did very well with breakfast. No fires, no problems."

Hannah smiled, but the smile came with tears. "Any change in her thinking?"

Angel sighed. The older woman was an excellent nurse, but not one to give false hope. "Not yet, but I try to remind her of what's important. No sign of those awful reporters, like we were afraid of. It's a blessing Miss Cordova doesn't know what they said about her."

Vegetable... Undisclosed mental illness... Pyromaniac... Probable Alzheimer's disease...

A grinding sound startled Hannah until she realized it was coming from her, from her clenched teeth. She deliberately relaxed her jaws. "I'll be out to see her in a few days, okay? Maybe by next week, we can bring her home for a visit without worrying. I really miss her."

"*Sí*. I think she misses you, too."

When Hannah hung up with Angel, she couldn't help a brief but murderous thought about Timothy and his tabloid betrayal. Until her sister could go back to her home and live in peace without being invaded and hounded by rabid reporters, and until Hannah was sure her mother would remain safely tucked away, Timothy wouldn't completely leave Hannah's mind — or fantasies of vengeance. Let the bastard stalk her if he had to, but he needed to leave her family alone. She might not shoot his worthless ass, but she did have a vampire for a friend now.

She tilted her head back and stared at a ceiling painted dark shades of taupe. She'd been in Zin's home for almost a week now, and soon she'd need to get back to Los Angeles, back to her family and her life. Her gaze fixed on a thread of a cobweb that must have been spun overnight, or Patricia would have nailed it with her dust mop.

Hannah sighed and turned her gaze back to the high-tech equipment. A screensaver showed a cross floating across the black screen, and she almost smiled at Zin's sense of humor. Instead tears stung at the back of her eyes.

"What happened, baby?" Patricia was standing in the doorway, rag in hand, eyes wide with concern. "Is everything okay?"

Hannah swallowed and nodded. "I just — uh, I needed to check on my mother. She's been sick."

"You should have said something! I would have had Zin take you to her, dangers or no." Patricia closed the gap between them and rested a hand on Hannah's wrist. "No need to keep your pains to yourself. We will help you with glad hearts."

"Th-Thanks." Hannah couldn't keep the older woman's gaze. Her dark eyes were too intense, like Zin's. "But right now, it's better if I stay away. There was a man, Timothy Mix — "

She bit back her words, but Patricia's genuine concern melted away her reserve. In minutes, the whole story came tumbling out—how she had trusted Timothy, what he had done, how her sister had been pestered out of her own home. And how she prayed the tabloids wouldn't find her mother.

"After that," she finished in a rush, "I vowed I'd never trust another human being besides my family and Britt. I'm too public. I can't afford the risk."

"I understand." As she spoke, Patricia led Hannah from the den to a couch along the far wall of the living room. "Very good thing our Zin isn't human, eh? He can escape your no-trust rule—and by now you've figured out he's as vulnerable as you when it comes to exposure." She opened the blinds, letting in the morning's sun. "Now sit and relax."

Hannah eased onto the comfortable couch and yawned in spite of herself. Her schedule was starting to get turned around. Night and day blurred together, and the sunlight felt odd on her skin. When Zin slept, she and Patricia kept the blinds open. Hannah usually went back to bed with him toward the approach of evening, just to get a little sleep. When they woke, if there was the teeniest bit of light left to the day, they wouldn't have known—they were too busy having incredible sex to care. By the time they got around to leaving the bedroom, without fail, Patricia had closed the blinds tightly before she headed to her own wing of the house.

"Do I need to tell you again that Zin's a good man?" Patricia asked quietly as she sat beside Hannah.

"No, no. Of course not." Hannah toyed with the hem of the white sundress Zin had bought her on one of his forays to Todos Santos. "It's just—thinking about Timothy and what happened to my family—"

Patricia shrugged. "Why don't you bring your family here? It's safe, and secret, and Zin would protect your loved ones just as he protects you."

Hannah felt stunned. The offer was so simple, so straightforward, yet it held so much meaning. "My mother has to have a nurse—and really, I've only known you and Zin for a week."

Eyebrow arched, Patricia studied her without comment.

"Okay." Hannah fidgeted. "So it seems a lot longer. But, still."

"Take all the time you need, baby. Zin will wait. Me, too. Though I'm less patient. Living for half a millennium increases his perspective, I think."

"How did you meet Zin?"

Patricia's usually bright expression darkened. "That's a sore story, even after all these years. But I'll tell you if you really want to know."

Hannah leaned toward Patricia. "If it hurts you too much, don't. But I would like to hear it when you're ready."

"Many years ago, when I was young like you, my husband and I began our journey north to the border with our three sons—to jobs, you know. Times were very hard in Mexico then. Still are." She trailed off, eyes distant and misty.

Knowing better than to press, Hannah waited.

The older woman seemed to gather herself, and she proceeded. "We didn't get far—we made it to Todos Santos and then..." Patricia's throat worked as she paused. "We stayed a few days, with my Miguel working odd jobs to feed us, then moved on. They were hiring further north, you see." Tears trickled down her face. She twisted her fingers together. "Crops, you know. Time for planting."

Dread stirred in Hannah's belly. She knew they were coming to the hard part, and she so hated that anything had wounded Patricia like this.

"We liked to walk at night, because it was cooler, but the night we left, a monsoon was stirring." Patricia's gaze shifted to the open blinds for a moment, then returned to meet Hannah's. "We looked for shelter on the dark highway, with all that cool wind—we could smell the ocean with each gust."

Patricia plunged ahead, speaking faster, freeing the words before her sorrow dammed them up again. "In the distance, we saw a glowing red light—"

No... Hannah battled back a wave of horror. *No, no, no...*

"Stop," Hannah whispered, her throat tight. "I know what comes next."

For a long few minutes, the two women sat holding each other's hands. Patricia's shoulders shook violently, then trembled, then settled back into her normal straight-backed posture.

"I don't know why they let me go," she murmured. "Those animals. I was unconscious much of the time, but I think I remember my husband and sons making a deal for my life."

Hannah's insides twisted. Here she had been mooning and moaning over a handful of ridiculous stories in a bunch of useless tabloids while this woman—this woman had real pain. "So, they were sacrificed."

Patricia pulled her hands free and stood, turning her back on Hannah. "I wish that were the case. My husband Miguel— possibly. Probably. No one has ever seen him. But my sons, they have been seen. They were made into *sirvientas sangre*, blood servants." Her shoulders started to shake. "As far as I know, they are still there, trapped forever in the Hotel Rojo."

The beast-man's growls rang in Hannah's mind like the church bell she had heard in the distance that awful night. The end of her index finger smarted, and she rubbed the tiny blood blister that just wouldn't go away. *I saw them,* she thought desperately. *The three young men through the crowd. The pale, hungry ones who held the sacrifice down for the goddess...oh, God. No wonder Patricia looked familiar to me when I first met her!*

"Why doesn't Zin rescue them?" Hannah leapt off the couch. "He brought his friends to spring me—why not save your boys?"

At this, Patricia turned back to Hannah. "You have a good heart, my newest baby, but what good would it do? Once a *sirvienta*, there are only two ways out—death by blood-starving, or finishing the change. I would rather my sons die than become what the *Lopos* are."

"Not acceptable! There must be another option." Hannah was surprised by her own desperation. "We have to do something."

Patricia actually mustered a chuckle. "It has been fifteen years, Hannah. And Zin, his friends, and I have talked circles around this issue. My sons and husband are dead to the world now, and dead to me. What lives in that hotel—those are not my children. Husks. Nothing more."

Husks who still look so much like you. Hannah wanted to scream, but she hugged Patricia instead. She even let Patricia lead her off to breakfast, but all the while her mind was working. She'd speak to Zin when he woke.

* * * * *

The moon was only just rising when Zin found his beloved standing over him, shaking him by the shoulders. The look on her face communicated one thing clearly—there would be no romance this evening, at least not now.

"You've slept long enough," she said urgently. "We need to talk about Patricia's sons. How can we get them out?"

Zin sat up, sleepy haze clearing from his thoughts. "She told you." He shook his head, banishing the last of the haze. "*Dios.* That's surprising. Since I found her out on the highway that night, she's kept it mostly to herself, except for strategizing with Creed and me."

"Whatever." Hannah gave his shoulders another impatient shake. "How do we save them?"

By all the gods, she was so beautiful, and even more so like this—indignation aroused, determined to go on a mission. He reached out and stroked her cheek. "There is no saving the boys, *mi alma*. If it could have been done, I would have seen to it years ago. They're blood servants, and the only way—"

"I've heard." Hannah sat heavily on the bed beside him. "Starvation, or full transformation to one of the *Lopos*. Are you sure?"

"Sadly, yes." Zin leaned forward and kissed her ear, her neck. "Your courage is admirable. I have no doubt you would storm Hotel Rojo, no matter that you've seen its many horrors."

"Patricia's sons are inside." Hannah rubbed her eyes and sniffed. "I can't stand that thought. My family means so much to me..."

And then she was holding onto him and crying, hard deep sobs from her very center.

Zin knew the terrible things she had witnessed, the many changes she had faced in her way of seeing the world, were catching up to her. He cradled her without comment, rocking her and kissing the top of her head.

No words could reduce the pain and confusion she felt. Only a steady presence, which Zin hoped he could be.

In time, she calmed enough to let him get up and bring her a washcloth. As he stood in front of her, she dabbed at her eyes and nose, and finally asked, "How do you stand it, all this tragedy?"

"It's not all darkness, Hannah." Zin bent forward and pressed his lips against her forehead. So soft. She tasted so sweet. "I saved Patricia and brought her here—and I'd like to think I helped save you. I've fought the *Lopos* many times and beaten them back—we all have. Sometimes, *Vampiros* win. Sometimes, I get to play the hero."

She gazed up at him. "The role suits you."

"Are you ready to venture out?" He cupped her chin and kept her face turned toward his. "It should be safe to try now—a good test. Creed's close by in case we need assistance. Would you like to see Todos Santos under my protection?"

Hannah nodded. "Yes. I'll put on one of the sundresses you bought me, and then you can get me out of here. Some fresh air would do me good."

Less than an hour later, Hannah found herself riding shotgun on a Harley Hog, hips thrust against Zin's muscled ass as they whipped toward town. He had on leather pants and his vest, along with sunglasses. No helmet.

I'm undead, Hannah. I don't need a helmet. You do, however. No, don't argue.

And so, she had on a classic Harley hat and her sundress. The sting of the cool night wind against her bare shoulders and legs made her wish she'd worn pants. She kept her arms tight around Zin's waist and her helmeted head against his shoulder as the big bike rumbled down the road.

High-tech vamps on bikes. Will wonders never cease?

Even in the fresh spring wind, she could smell him. Basic, earthy, and spicy in that oh-so-male way. For all of her singing success and newly world-wise ways, Hannah had never ridden on a motorcycle—especially not with an undead bad boy. The thrum of the Harley's authoritative engine sent shivers all through her body, and the heat—damn. She felt like she was riding a huge chrome and black vibrator. Her nipples tightened against Zin's back, and her pussy tingled each time he moved or revved the bike for a little extra speed.

This kind of freedom—she never thought she'd feel it again. It was better than being an anonymous girl back in Arizona. Better, even than belting Karaoke in some dark, smoky bar. It was perfection—with horsepower. And a hunk at the handlebars.

The faster they moved, the more Hannah felt cut loose from everything that burdened her.

Does this help Zin, too? Can he be free of his pains and worries while he's driving this monster?

As if in response, Zin gunned the bike, and they shot forward. Hannah's heart drummed in harmony with the Harley. When she opened her eyes, the wind bit into her lashes, bringing tears. Night prismed around her, and for a few moments, she imagined that she was flying.

...Soaring through night sky...

...White feathers ruffling...

Her vision was so sharp, and the regal jaguar was so close. Fire blazed from a thousand pyres, reaching from sand to sky. People were singing, loud and strong, not mournful. Raging, angry. They sang to rid themselves of demons, to reaffirm life and the right to be free.

As if from great height, Hannah could see a woman inside a circle of literally thousands of people with heads bowed. The woman's hands lifted, and flames shot from her very palms.

Hannah gasped.

The woman was dressed like an Aztec deity, but in a much older style than the pretenders in Hotel Rojo. They would quail before such a being as this. Hannah felt no fear, though. Only awe, and wonder, and a deep sense that she knew the dark-skinned, white-haired, fire-throwing priestess.

"Where are the daughters of Omecihuatl?" the woman chanted in a language Hannah didn't speak, but understood. "Come, Lady of Duality, goddess of good-evil, light-darkness. Creator and destroyer, we call to you in our time of need. Send us your daughters. We cry to the daughters of Omecihuatl. Free us. Free us!"

Hannah flapped her wings, dodging pillars of fire, mind swirling with confusion. She stared down at the woman — and recognized her with a start.

"Mom?" she said to the wind, doubling her grip on Zin. Her blood-blistered finger stung, and the vision blew away like so much mist. She was Hannah again, on the Harley, clinging tight to her rebel with fangs.

Once more, the motion and rumble of the bike caught her attention, and she plunged further into sheer sensory enjoyment. The vision strengthened and amused her. How wonderful to see her mother healthy again, to see her fierce and in control, wielding fire instead of setting useless little blazes and babbling about things no one understood.

Maybe this time, this place – this man – are magic. Maybe this is the magic I've needed.

For the briefest moment, she imagined her family relaxing at Zin's villa, tended by Patricia and Angel. She imagined herself joined forever with Zin, living and singing her heart out every night, riding from concert to concert on the back of his majestic Harley.

"Stop it," she muttered aloud, and forced her attention back to the moment.

Damn, but Zin felt good, solid as a post in her arms. The bike hummed between her thighs, making her clit burn and swell. Even the stinging wind became a thrill, sensitizing her skin, making her ache for Zin to rub his hands over every inch of her flesh.

By the time they reached Todos Santos, Hannah was so horny she could barely contain herself. Zin drove lazily through the paved streets, avoiding potholes and pointing out the sites in the town that was sandwiched between the Sierra Laguna Mountain Range and the Pacific Ocean. There were quaint stores in the Historic District and most buildings throughout the town were whitewashed or painted in a combination of vivid hues. According to Zin the town was a thriving artists' colony, boasting over a dozen art galleries.

Neon lights from nightclubs pulsed in the near darkness and music flowed out to the streets. Mariachi, modern Mexican music, and even jazz…the town throbbed with a life of its own. Pulsed and throbbed, like her body as she rode behind her night warrior.

Hannah enjoyed sharing everything with Zin, but when they passed a church, it brought back the memory of the church bell she'd heard the night she was drawn to Hotel Rojo. For a moment in time, her blood ran cold and the blister on her finger ached with sudden intensity.

Moments later, Zin parked the bike at the mouth of an alley, facing a small bar, and she gratefully dragged her mind from memories of the Hotel Rojo. Residual heat from the daytime sun rose from the pavement in misty waves, making the bar seem surreal. The neon sign above the hovel blinked off and on, reds and blacks announcing *El Zapata Rojo*. The Red Shoe.

Hannah's body hummed from the ride, and her skin ached. Both nipples felt like hot rocks against the soft cotton of her dress, and her pussy throbbed. She was nearly panting with desire, but she pulled off her helmet and tried to maintain her composure. Before she could get her bearings, Zin was gone—as if he'd vanished into thin air. Hannah startled, realizing he was standing beside her now.

"Don't *do* that," she muttered. "It rattles my brain."

Zin gave her a secretive smile, took her helmet, came back and climbed on the bike behind her.

"Go on," he said in his delicious bass rumble, scooting up until his leather-clad erection pressed against her ass. "Grab the handle bars and don't let go."

Hannah spread her arms wide, reached up, and grabbed the leather grips.

"Put your feet on the pegs," Zin instructed.

This was harder.

Hannah scooted her dress around and finally maneuvered her legs until her feet rested comfortably on the metal and rubber stops. Her dress barely covered her underwear, and with her legs so wide and high, she could smell her own arousal.

"Can you see the door clearly?" Zin asked in low, sensual tones. He slipped his hands forward and cupped Hannah's breasts.

She groaned before managing a quiet, "Yes."

"Keep your eyes open." He pinched her nipples through her dress, sending shocks along her pleasure centers. "Don't blink." He pinched her again, harder, then rolled the sensitive flesh between his fingers.

Hannah struggled to keep her eyes open and on the door. What if someone came out? What if someone saw them?

"They'd be jealous, wouldn't they?" Zin laughed and tweaked her nipples again and again, making Hannah shudder. Damn him, reading her mind like that. She wasn't really mad, just revved up and a little nervous. Some embarrassed. A lot turned on.

Here she was, sitting on a motorcycle's leather seat, legs hiked up, arms spread wide, with a man—a vampire—fondling her breasts in public.

Someone *could* see. But somehow, she thought no one would. Zin didn't seem the sort to share.

The bar door opened, and two men came out, stumbling and laughing. Zin didn't let up on her nipples. Hannah's cheeks burned as hot as her clit.

The men staggered off into the night without ever turning their attention toward the alley.

Hannah took a deep breath of the steamy, fresh mist. Now and again, a cool ocean breeze blew foggy swirls around the bike. Zin leaned forward and nibbled on her neck, and she moaned despite her best efforts to be quiet.

Her eyelids fluttered from the pleasure.

"Eyes open, Hannah. You're going to choose for me tonight."

"What?"

Zin's right hand slid from her breast and traveled down her belly. In seconds, he had slipped his fingers under her bunched dress and into her underwear.

"So wet," he murmured as he massaged her pussy, slipping in and out of her folds, teasing, not quite touching her clit. "I love the way you feel. I love how you smell, Hannah. Are you watching the bar?"

"Uh-huh," she stammered. Her throat tightened. She was an inch from coming, right here in front of anyone who cared to look.

"Good. Now, watch hard." With that, Zin slid two fingers against her clit and rubbed slow circles.

Hannah bucked almost immediately. Heat rose from her toes to her head, spreading in all directions. Zin's fingers seemed to vibrate like the bike. With one hand, he pinched her breasts through her dress. With the other, he kept a relentless, moving pressure between her legs. Right on the spot. The perfect, hot, aching spot.

"Zin," she whispered. "Damn. Zin!"

"Keep watching the bar."

Fighting with all her strength and what little attention she could muster, Hannah strained her eyes to keep staring through the mists. All she could feel were Zin's hands, busy driving her insane. All she could hear was the rasp of his hot breath in her ear. He made her tingle. He made her want to scream. Over the past week she had learned how to control her tendency to glow when she climaxed, but right now she was about to totally lose it.

Helpless, she came with a shuddering cry just as the nightclub's door opened. Two men and a woman came out together, chattering and talking.

"People," Hannah choked, still jerking from the aftershocks of her orgasm.

Zin laughed softly, giving her a new round of jerks and chills. "Good. Thank you."

He slipped his fingers out of her panties, let go of her breast, and kissed her neck. "Wait here. I'll bring them to us."

Hannah almost yelled from surprise. "What are you talking about?" she hissed as Zin sauntered away into the mists. "Come back here, you vampire brat!"

He did come back, only seconds later, with the two men and the woman trailing behind him like obedient puppies. One by one, he lined them up against the alley wall, just out of sight of the bar.

Hannah struggled off the Harley and stood beside him. "What's wrong with them?"

"Nothing. They're mesmerized."

Both men were well-muscled and dressed in jeans and white T-shirts. The woman beside them—she was a beauty with her dark skin and flowing black hair. Zin sniffed at the men. "Tequila. Good."

Next, he sniffed the woman's neck, and Hannah stiffened at seeing his mouth so close to her skin. "And this one—wine coolers. Not as good, but much better than beer."

"Are you going to bite her?" Hannah could barely rein in her jealousy. She had an absurd urge to slap the woman until she woke up, then scream *Vampire! Run!*

"What would you like me to do, *mi alma*?" Zin's voice had that maddening, teasing quality. "You chose these. You tell me."

Hannah didn't hesitate. "You can bite the men, but leave her alone."

"As you will." Zin's laugh made Hannah want to slap him next.

Instead, she watched, fascinated, as he fed on the men. So fast, so neat. They didn't seem to mind or suffer, and he healed their wounds the moment he finished. Then, he spoke in low tones to the three of them, using a mix of a language she didn't understand and more modern Spanish. She thought she caught the words, "fuck," "three-way," and "all night."

Then, Zin nudged the three away from the wall. They wandered through the mists, back to the main road. In seconds, they were as alert as before, only touching each other and giggling in a most aroused way.

"What did you do?" Hannah put her hands on her hips. "Send them off to have wild sex?"

"Exactly." Zin's killer grin looked twice as wicked in the blinking light from the neon sign across the street. "Their reward for being my dinner."

Hannah shook her head. "You're incorrigible."

"It's better than intense, yes?" He tweaked a strand of her dark hair. "Can't a guy catch a break?"

"All right, bad boy." She reached up and tugged at a lock of his long hair in return. "Just stick to sucking male necks. Skip the women."

Zin chuckled and gave her a long delicious kiss.

Minutes later they were back on the bike and rolling toward home, only Hannah made Zin stop twice to relieve her excitement with his oh-so-skilled fingers.

Chapter Ten
Late Night

Night breezes chilled Hannah's skin during the ride home on the back of Zin's Harley. The hog growled between her thighs and his long hair whipped about her cheeks, the slight sting like moonlight kisses. Sated for the time being, she wrapped her arms tighter around his waist and snuggled her cheek against his back, the best she could while wearing her helmet.

Her pussy continued to throb against the seat, and she imagined the leather must be covered with her juices, as soaked as her panties were. With every swerve and turn of the bike, her pussy ached that much more. She slid her hand down to Zin's crotch and squeezed his cock, smiling as it jerked against her hand. She imagined herself in front of him, his cock sliding in and out of her, fucking her as he drove the rest of the way back.

By the time Zin and Hannah arrived at his home, she was so hot for him that she could hardly stand it. The orgasms he'd given her on the way had done nothing to feed the hunger she had for him. She wasn't sure what would...if her hunger for him would ever truly be satisfied.

After he parked the bike and closed the garage doors, she gave his cock one last squeeze and dismounted. He followed, swinging his long leg over the bike and then gave her that dark, sexy look that made her legs weak. He rubbed his cock through his pants and said, "You're in trouble now, woman."

"I am?" Butterflies zipped through her belly at the promise in his gaze as he gave a slow nod.

When she pulled off the helmet, he took it from her and set it aside, then scooped her up. Before she had a chance to catch her breath, he flung her over his shoulder, causing air to whoosh from her lungs, and blood to rush to her head. She laughed in surprise, a sense of pure joy washing through her. How she enjoyed this man that she'd grown to trust and to care for, maybe even to…

Hannah's thoughts scattered as Zin slipped his hand beneath her dress and slid it up her thigh. "You've been a bad girl, teasing me the way you have." He caressed her ass through the silky underwear while he walked into the house and down a short hall. "I'm sending you straight to bed."

She laughed again. "And you'll tuck me in?"

He gave a low rumble. "I'll be tucking *in to* you, all right."

With a giggle she swatted his delicious buttocks and then squeezed them with both hands. While he walked the hard muscles flexed beneath her palms and she had the sudden urge to bite his ass. Maybe she would, first chance she got.

The next thing she knew they were in his bedroom and Zin was sliding her down his chest. Her sandals clicked on tile when her feet reached the floor and then she was looking up at him. In that moment the memory of the day he'd brought her to his home washed over her—a sense of déjà vu. Only this time she was in his bedroom…and totally in love with him.

She swallowed back the nearly overwhelming rush of fear combined with unbelievable happiness. Fear at making herself so vulnerable by falling in love with him, and happiness at finding a man she could trust, a man who would never hurt her.

A man she could love.

The thought stunned her, but she knew she couldn't deny it.

Zin held Hannah close, studying her features and watching the play of emotions as he absorbed what he had captured in her thoughts. Even though it frightened her, he had her trust and her love.

Hannah loved him.

The realization filled him with such joy, joy that he had not experienced in over five centuries, before Aki had died. More so—somehow he loved Hannah more intensely, more fiercely than he had loved Aki.

Hannah trembled within his embrace and placed her head against his chest, her arms tight around his waist. The pulse of blood through her veins and the beating of her heart throbbed throughout his body. He had tasted her blood once, when she had given it freely in order to heal him. Now her blood called to him louder than ever, a beautiful song that washed over him. As much as he'd wanted to have the ultimate bonding with Hannah—to sink his fangs into her sweet flesh and drink from her—he knew it had to be her choice.

It was only a matter of time before she would want the blood-sharing as much as he did. She was his.

But at this moment he sensed her need to come to terms with her emotions, and he was certain she wouldn't be pleased that he had listened in on her thoughts. He forced himself to withdraw for the moment, to give her time to realize her love for him was real.

He lowered his head and brushed his lips over her hair as he massaged her shoulders. "My Hannah. *Mi alma, mi corazón.*"

"Make love to me, Zin." She tilted her head up to look at him, her golden-green eyes wide, her conflicting emotions so easy to read within their depths. "Make love to me," she whispered again.

He stroked her hair away from her face and smiled. "With all my heart."

Hannah's world condensed into this one precious moment. Nothing existed in her mind but the man before her, the man who now owned her heart and soul. The sound of his breathing, the pounding of her heart, the thrills in her belly—everything whirled and surged within her, so powerfully that it almost made her dizzy with its intensity.

She bit her lip as Zin pushed the straps of her sundress from her shoulders. He kissed the places he bared, magnifying the wild tingling sensations throughout her body. He eased the dress off, slowly sliding the cotton fabric down until her breasts were freed.

"In all my years," he said as he lightly brushed each nipple with the back of his hand, "I've never known such feelings as I have for you."

She swallowed back the rush of trepidation and excitement. A part of her wanted Zin to tell her he loved her, yet a part was still afraid. Even though she was in love with him, she didn't know what would happen in the future. She just wanted to celebrate the here and now.

Zin let her dress fall and it swirled in a white cloud to her feet, leaving her standing before him, clad only in her panties. She could barely breathe as he skimmed his hands along her sides to the gentle flare of her hips. He knelt before her and hooked his fingers in the sides of her silky underwear and slid them down to her ankles. She stepped out and kicked the dress and panties away.

"I can never get enough of you." He groaned as he grasped her hips and nuzzled the curls of her mound. "Your scent, your taste…everything about you."

Before she could respond, he flicked his tongue along her slit and she moaned as she felt her moisture flowing over his tongue. Her body was ready for him…yet she wasn't so sure her heart was.

"Mine," he murmured, his voice rumbling with possessiveness.

Yours, her mind echoed.

He gripped her hips tighter and nipped the soft flesh of her mound. She felt the scrape of his incisors and her heartbeat picked up a pace. What would it be like to have him slide his fangs into the vein at her neck, and for him to take her blood? Strangely the thought was intriguing now, rather than disquieting. After watching him feed on the two men, she had the odd urge to share that experience with him. Was he bewitching her in the same way he controlled the men and the woman?

"Do you want me to bewitch you, Hannah?" Zin's bass rumble startled and thrilled her.

Hannah imagined herself passive, unable to resist him, completely open to whatever he chose to do to her.

"Would I be aware?" she whispered. "Would I remember?"

His laugh was deep and rich. "I could arrange that. If you want it. But realize, it would last until we're finished. I wouldn't release you until I climaxed—and that could take a long, long time."

Heart pounding, Hannah took a few breaths. Then, she murmured, "Do it. Do it, and then please me until I can't stand it any more."

Zin raised himself above her and gazed into her eyes. He seemed to hover, and her mind drifted for a moment.

With the force of irrefutable command, she heard him say, "You'll stay with me. Stay aware. You can speak, but not resist. Whatever I say, you'll comply. Now, relax."

Hannah felt her muscles go completely limp. Her entire body felt more relaxed than she could ever remember being—except for her pussy. That was tight, and throbbing, and utterly alive.

Zin didn't make her wait. She could feel his mind brushing against her, feel his thoughts twining with hers. Being careful. Making sure she didn't change her mind.

"You may touch me, if you wish," he whispered, his breathing shallow, as he knelt again at her feet. "My hair. My shoulders. Nothing else."

"Take me," she murmured, hearing the languid desire in her own words.

Growling, Zin buried his face against her folds, banishing all thoughts save for the feel of his tongue against her clit. Hannah gave a soft cry and clenched her hands in his hair, both to steady herself, and to press him tighter against her pussy. With the same intensity he did everything in life, he sucked and licked at her clit. She wanted to buck and thrash, but she could only moan.

Zin spread her legs wide, so wide. As wide as she could stand. She was completely open to him now, her clit throbbing and swollen as he gently pulled it in and out of his lips.

Hannah wondered if she could die from too much pleasure. If she could explode.

Warmth spread throughout her body as he continued, flicking the pulsing center with his tongue again and again, until she came so fast her head spun and her body shuddered against his face.

He pulled back, eyes hooded as he gazed at her. "What do you think, *mi alma*? Could you be a vampire's woman? Could you stand to be pleasured like this, day after day, year after year, century after century?"

"I don't know," she whispered truthfully.

Zin casually slipped a finger into her channel and pushed it deep.

Hannah moaned louder. Her thoughts stayed relaxed, like her muscles—it was a wonder she could stand. The universe seemed centered on the place he was touching her. One finger, and one finger only. In and out. In and out.

He kept his gaze fixed on her face, kept her legs splayed wide, giving him full access. In and out, in and out with that finger. Her nipples felt so hard, so tight. Her clit was throbbing again.

"Come for me," he ordered, pushing so deep his hand slapped against her folds.

Helpless against his commands, Hannah exploded with her orgasm. It felt like a wave of fire, moving out from her pussy, then up, up across her nipples, to her neck, to her face.

She had never felt anything so splendid, not in her entire life.

She was still trembling when he stopped, slipped his finger out, and laid a soft kiss on her mound. Then he began to move up her body, kissing her flat belly and flicking his tongue over the jaguar ring at her navel. She'd had such a powerful orgasm that she was surprised she hadn't lost control and burst into blue flame.

"You're so beautiful, so perfect." His voice touched her just like his lips and fingers. "A pleasure, made just for me."

Fire licked Hannah's body wherever his mouth rested in a brief and sensuous kiss. The more aroused he became, the darker and more dangerous he looked.

And here she was, helpless. Completely at a vampire's mercy.

Zin worked his way up to her breast and gently bit each nipple with a growl.

Hannah cried out with pleasure as he teased her, alternating between flicks of his tongue and nips with his fangs. All the while, he kept one leather-clad leg against her pussy, rubbing up and down. She lost count of her little orgasms—and her big ones. How could her body just keep responding? What kind of power did this man really have?

Who cares? So long as he never stopped.

When he finally reached her lips, he slipped his hand into her hair and smiled down at her. His eyes were blacker than ever, a smoldering midnight with the flash of stars. And then he kissed her, slow and deep. She tasted him, tasted herself upon her lips and tongue.

"Like honey, but better," he murmured, the sound of his voice giving her a new round of shuddering chills. His leather-covered thigh pressed hard against her clit, making her throb as he kissed her again and again.

"I want you to come for me again, *mi corazón*. Come when I kiss you next."

Hannah felt her body tense in response to his instruction. He rocked the rough-smooth leather against her clit, and buried his tongue in her mouth as he held onto her, tight. He smelled of night air and essence of male and felt hard and warm against her body.

She came with a racking tremble, moaning her pleasure into his mouth. He drank the sound like he might drink her blood, growling his pleasure.

He eased away from her and held her gaze again. "Your turn," he said quietly. "Touch me any way you would like—for now."

Immediately, Hannah moved her hands beneath his vest. "My turn," she murmured as she pushed the vest from his shoulders and let it slide down his arms to the floor.

"I want your mouth on me," he told her, and Hannah's mesmerized mind and body couldn't wait to comply. She had been thinking exactly the same thing.

Moving with the same languor with which she spoke, Hannah knelt on the cool tile, her hands upon the fastenings of his leather pants. Her fingers trembled as she unsnapped them and pulled the zipper down. She pushed the pants down to his thighs and his cock slipped free.

"Mine," she said as she cupped his balls and stroked his cock. She looked up at her man, her vampire, and met his gaze.

Zin saw no mischief in Hannah's eyes, and no stupor. Instead she was almost solemn, as if taking care of an awesome responsibility. He was tempted to dip into her thoughts again, wanting to share everything with her, but this time he held back.

Stay in control, man. Don't lose it.

Her gaze remained focused on him as she caressed the length of his erection, and then she slid her mouth over the head. Zin groaned as she swirled her tongue over his cock and took him deep, deeper than she ever had before. His pants slid further down his legs and he swore his toes curled in his boots. Her scent filled his senses and her blood called to him. He imagined himself drinking from her, completing the bonding that would make her his forever.

The fierce ache in his loins grew, spreading from his balls and cock throughout his chest. He felt like the top of his head would lift off as relief approached, fast and white-hot.

Gods, what a woman!

There was no holding back. Not with her.

Zin nearly pierced his tongue with his fangs as his fluid spurted into her mouth and down her throat. She drank from him, never taking her eyes from his.

Almost instantly, the languor of enchantment left her. When she slipped his cock from her mouth, she sat on her haunches and watched him kick off his boots and strip his pants the rest of the way off.

"I didn't think you'd let me go that fast," she teased. "I thought it would take hours."

In an easy movement he scooped her up and held her naked body against his. "You make me impatient."

Carefully, he laid her on the bed then slid between her thighs and braced his hands to either side of her breasts. Gods, the look on her face. The exhausted satisfaction. The already-increasing desire.

"You are the other half of my soul." Zin swallowed back the emotion that threatened to overpower him as he looked down at his Eternal Mate. "I've been looking for you for over five centuries."

"I've dreamed of you for the last sixteen years." Hannah caught a lock of his hair and drew him closer to her. "Always it was you who came to me in my sleep, you who chased away my nightmares. I think I've even been singing to you, for you, my whole life."

"I will always be there for you, *mi alma*." He brushed his lips over her forehead. "I love you, Hannah."

She froze, for a moment unable to believe that he'd said it. He loved her, he would always be there for her. She opened her mouth to tell him that she loved him, too, but the words stuck in her throat.

I'm not ready. Hannah fought against giving her all to him. *Not yet*. By telling him she loved him, she would be giving her heart totally away.

Zin didn't seem to notice her lack of response. He kissed her, letting his tongue slide into her mouth at the same time he placed his cock at the opening of her channel. Hannah wrapped her legs around his hips and arched up, but he wouldn't slide into her the way she wanted him to.

With a rasping sigh he moved his mouth from hers and kissed the corner of her mouth. "I need to taste all of you, *querida*." Sweat dripped from his brow and ran along the side of his handsome face. "I promise you only pleasure. Will you trust me that much, like you did earlier, when you let me put you under enchantment?"

The dreams came back to her in a rush. He had called her *querida* in her dreams, had been poised over her just like he was now. Would he disappear if she said no?

Did she want to say no? How completely did she want to give herself to this man? This vampire?

The answer came to her, sharp and clear. Right now, more than anything, she wanted to give him everything. Wanted to take all that he offered. She trusted him with her heart and soul and knew that he wouldn't take more than she was prepared to give him.

"Yes." The word came out softly at first and then she said it with more force as he continued to hold her gaze. "*Yes*."

A sexy, predatory smile curved the corner of his mouth, giving her a glimpse of his fangs. For a second she felt a stab of fear, but then it was replaced by confidence that her man would never hurt her.

"You will have no regrets. That I promise."

With that, Zin thrust his cock deep inside her and she gasped her pleasure. Several small orgasms shuddered through her as he drove into her with long, deliberate strokes. Her moans became louder and she found herself close to begging for his bite.

Never stopping in his thrusts, Zin lowered his head and nuzzled the curve of her neck. Hannah tensed as she felt the scrape of fangs and then cried out at the brief stab of burning pain as he sank his incisors deep. Immediate pleasure followed the pain, intense ecstasy that soared throughout her body and soul. His bite created some kind of connection between them, and she felt as if she could feel his pleasure mixed with hers.

She had never known such complete ecstasy as she did at that moment. The feel of Zin's fangs in her neck and her blood flowing from her body into his...the feel of his cock driving in and out of her...his sweat-coated body rubbing against hers... It was so exquisite it was almost too much to bear. A total possession. A total sharing. Tears burned her eyes and she almost wept from the sweet, sweet sensations.

Zin's mind expanded as Hannah's blood flowed into his mouth and over his tongue. He drank deeply of the gift she offered him. The copper-rich elixir of her life tasted so incredible, so perfect, he knew he would never get his fill, could never get enough of her. He growled and drew more, needing her blood, needing that complete melding of their bodies and their souls.

He thrust harder, drank harder, his mind whirling, intoxicated by the ambrosia filling him. She tasted of light and fire, sweet and pure.

"Don't stop," Hannah pleaded. "Don't stop!"

Hannah was flying, her mind sailing in some other place and time. She was locked in her dream world where he had come to her again and again. Finally she knew what would make him stay. He had wanted her body, her heart, her soul — and her blood.

Warmth spread over her, a sweet rush of fire licking and kissing every inch of her flesh as her satisfaction came in a hard rush, even as her blood rushed into his mouth. She screamed in pleasure and release with the most powerful orgasm she'd ever had in her life. Misty colors and streamers of light blurred before her eyes and she felt all at once powerful, yet helpless. Broken into countless pieces, yet complete.

"Don't stop," she mumbled again, wanting the sensation to last forever.

Zin filled himself so fully with his Eternal Mate's blood that he almost couldn't stop himself.

I'm losing control. I need to slow down, stop.

But he couldn't.

His climax came swift and sudden and he raised his head and growled with the force of his orgasm. Her blood raged in his veins while his cock pumped his fluid inside her core. He felt more powerful, more invincible than he had ever felt in his life as an immortal.

Hannah bucked and moaned, squeezing her thighs against his hips until he was thoroughly and completely drained. Then, she went limp. Exhausted. Satiated. Perfection for both of them.

He bent his head to nuzzle his woman. With a swipe of his tongue he sealed the wound on her shoulder, then licked at the rivulets of blood that had spilled down her neck, over her shoulder and onto the bed. Drops of her sweet essence were bright crimson against the turquoise sheet.

Hannah didn't move. She didn't even twitch. He could barely hear the beating of her heart.

Zin raised himself back up and his heart nearly failed him when he saw how pale she was. Had he taken too much blood? Had he started the process of transformation?

Hannah's eyelids fluttered open. She smiled at him with a dazed expression. neither here nor there, as if she was caught in some other place and time.

"*Dios.*" Zin's heart sank. Cold dread filled his belly.

The truth could scarcely be denied, though he wanted to erase it with all of his spirit and strength.

"Hannah," he choked, wishing he could lower himself beside her and die. "I'm so sorry. *Mi alma. I – I didn't mean to. I would never – not without your consent –*"

But curse him to the fate of the *Lopos*, he had. He had!

Without her knowledge or permission, he had started the process of transformation.

Self-loathing swelled in his chest. If he didn't complete what he had begun, she would become a blood servant, a pale existence of her former vibrant self.

That was unacceptable. Unthinkable.

And yet, if he pushed ahead, she'd wake a *Vampiro*, locked into an existence she hadn't asked for — an existence she might have rejected, if he'd given her a choice.

He could let her die, yes, he could do that. Zin's mind worked feverishly. He *would* die with her then, at the second death of his Eternal Mate. There would be no third chance, not that he deserved one.

But killing Hannah — equally unacceptable. Beyond unthinkable.

He had to finish it. He had to. She could kill him later if she wanted, and he wouldn't much blame her.

For now, though, there was no going back.

Chapter Eleven
Midnight

For what seemed like time on end, Zin stayed frozen above Hannah.

He couldn't make himself finish, and he couldn't make himself give up.

You're worthless, aren't you? His thoughts pounded him as harshly as any renegade *Vampiro*. *How could you do this to her?*

His hands were braced to either side of her chest, his cock still buried deep within her core. Fury and pain at his stupidity, at the depth of his betrayal of Hannah gripped his heart with an icy fist.

Little by little, Hannah slipped further into the change. She stared at the ceiling with unseeing eyes, lost in another existence, another world. A world she hadn't chosen to enter.

For the first time in his many centuries of existence as a vampire, Zin felt a regret so deep that it crippled him. Never had he turned a human without his or her consent. Never had he crossed that line.

Until now. With the woman I love.

He had never doubted that one day she would choose to join him, to become an immortal. He had been certain they would live their lives together for eternity — and that she would do so because she loved him.

But now he had taken that choice from her, and he knew she would hate him for it. She had trusted him and he had failed her.

"I am so sorry, *mi alma*," he repeated again and again. A heavy sigh shook his massive body and he brushed his lips across Hannah's cold forehead. "One day I hope you will forgive me. I have to finish now. Please understand."

Her eyelids fluttered and then closed as he trailed his lips down her cheek toward the curve of her neck. The smell of sex mingled with the sweet scent of her blood. Her pulse had slowed, each beat sluggish.

Zin's gut clenched when he reached the marks from his fangs, marks he had given her just moments before. This time when he slid his incisors into her flesh there was no pleasure in it. He drank of her blood, draining her to the point where she was no longer a living being.

From his bite—from being nearly drained—she was on the very brink of becoming *Vampiro*—and female *Vampiro* were nothing to be trifled with, especially during and immediately following the change. During the blood-madness, Hannah could very well take off his head.

But first he had to feed her his own blood, or she would pass into the afterlife.

When he had sealed the wounds in her neck, he rose up and slid his cock from her core. As he used his fangs to tear into the flesh on the inside of his wrist, he straddled her. The pain from the bite was brief and he paid little attention to it as he brought his wrist to her lips and forced it against her mouth. Her lips were closed and his blood ran down her chin and onto the delicate skin of her neck.

She moaned, her eyelids still shut tight. But then her tongue flicked out and she tasted his blood. Without conscious knowledge of what she was doing, Hannah's hunger was kindled. Zin could see it happening, like a flush of heat rising from her belly to her head. She began to suck from his wrist, tentatively at first, but then stronger and stronger. He gave all he could to her and then some. He was almost to the point of passing out when he finally took his wrist from her.

"Be strong," he muttered. "Survive."

She made a soft sound of protest at losing his wrist, her blood-smeared lips forming a small pout. But then her features relaxed and he knew she was sliding into a deep, healing sleep. When she woke it would not be easy for her, but she would now be *Vampiro*. An immortal. One of the most powerful females on the planet.

And she would probably hunt him down like a worthless hound dog and chew him to pieces.

Zin closed the wound at his wrist then licked blood from her lips, her chin and her throat. He tasted her sweet essence mixed with his, but this time it brought him no satisfaction. Only grief. He knew he might be tasting her for the last time.

When he finished, he eased off Hannah and stood beside the bed. She lay there so quietly, so peacefully, not knowing she was now one of the undead. She would wake to an alien world, to hungers and pains she would not understand.

After he covered her naked body with a sheet, he put his clothing back on and then began pacing the length of the room. He should send for Creed, at least. Go and wake Patricia. Something. He might not be able to manage Hannah on his own, keep her safe until the madness passed. He clenched and unclenched his hands as his boots thumped against the tiled floor. He was weak from having given Hannah so much of his blood, but at that moment it meant nothing to him, other than the fact it might impair him from protecting her.

He glanced back to Hannah and something on her hand caught his attention. A blood blister on her index finger—tiny, but vivid red against her pale skin.

Before his disbelieving eyes, it began growing, spreading slowly to cover the entire pad of her finger.

Zin came to an abrupt stop before the bed. His heart thudded as his senses told him all he needed to know. Still he caught her limp wrist and rubbed his thumb over the blister. Why hadn't he seen the mark? How could he have missed it—

unless it hadn't grown so large until she was turned. He had no experience with that. Creed would know.

"Damn!"

His blood ran cold.

Like Patricia's sons, Hannah had signed away her soul when she signed the "guestbook" at the Hotel Rojo, and now, he had changed her. Now she would become a beacon for the bastards, calling them down on her like wild animals. She was *Vampiro* now. Twice as attractive. Twice as desirable. They would stop at nothing to take her. That much, Zin *did* know, even without Creed telling him.

The *Lopos* would come for her, yes, and soon. They would be relentless until they had her—unless he killed them all and cancelled her debt. Unless he found a way into Hotel Rojo, took on wards that ten covens couldn't break, and destroyed that fucking Book of Blood.

He ground his teeth and wave after wave of fury rolled over him. He released her arm, bent down and tore off a section of the sheet beneath her, then turned and strode from the room, carrying the swath of sheet full of her sweet scent and juices— and more importantly, drops of her blood. It was likely he was going to his death, but he wouldn't stop until the Book was torn to pieces, the beasts were dead, and Hannah was forever safe from the *Lopos*.

Zin stuffed the sheet into his back pocket and headed toward the kitchen. When he reached it, Patricia was drawing a package of frozen human blood from out of the freezer. She was in her bathrobe, her dark hair poking up this way and that, and her mouth pursed into a frown.

"You turned her," she stated as she brought the blood to the counter and began to make the concoction. "I can't believe you did that. You turned her—and she didn't want it. Zin. *Dios.* Fuck you for doing such a thing!"

Zin didn't need to ask her how she knew. Somehow Patricia always knew when something was wrong. He ran his hand over his face and into his hair. "Yeah. I screwed up. Big time."

"Screwed up?" Patricia snorted. "That doesn't touch it, baby. Doesn't even put a finger on it."

He didn't want to stand around discussing anything—he needed to take care of business. But he was so drained from feeding Hannah that common sense told him he should drink Patricia's remedy before taking on the *Lopos*. He should feed on fresh human blood, too.

Patricia squeezed the blood from the pouch into a tall glass. "Where are you going now?"

"I need to feed." *And then I'm going out. For good.*

She opened a jar on the countertop, took a handful of mixed herbs, and chucked them into the glass. "What else?"

"Nothing." Zin's frustration mounted and he wanted to ram his fist into the kitchen wall. "Check in on Hannah. She'll need you when she wakes."

Patricia grabbed the bottle of tequila from next to the herb jar and poured a good dose into the glass of blood. After mixing the concoction, she handed the glass to Zin. "Don't leave. Hannah needs you. She'll need *you* more than ever when she wakes."

He downed the vile mixture and slammed the glass onto the countertop. It shattered, the bloody glass scattering across the granite surface.

"I'll be back," he lied as he strode out of the kitchen and through the door into the garage. "Go to Ops and call Creed."

Patricia didn't try to stop him.

The door closed behind him with a loud thump. He headed toward the collection arranged on the garage wall and began arming himself with every weapon he could. One gun in the back of his pants, one in each holster, knives strapped to his legs and tucked into his boots. A small detonator and a few land mines he stashed in his pockets, and then he strapped on his long-sword and checked the one sheathed on the motorcycle.

When he was armed to the teeth he opened the garage door at the same time he mounted his Harley, then roared into the night.

* * * * *

Colors and light swirled around Hannah as she soared through clouds and dark sky. She flapped her wings then caught a cool wind and gently spiraled with it toward the ground. The night smelled of rain and ocean breezes, of life…but also of death.

A smell that chilled her, pierced her like daggers to her heart.

Below she saw her jaguar, but he was more distant now, as if separated by some invisible barrier. Fear rose in her throat as she pumped her wings, trying to get to him, but she was pulled farther and farther away.

In the next second she stood at the center of a dark circle and tilted her face to the sky. Thousands of people surrounded her, on their knees and praying as words spilled from her lips, words in an ancient language that somehow she understood.

"Hear me, Omecihuatl. Your daughters have come."

In the crowd below, two women stepped forward. They looked familiar, but Hannah didn't have time to focus on who they were. Priestesses, *some part of her mind noted.* Servants of the light. We are all servants of the light!

Britt's voice cut in, as if from great distance. "What the fuck is this?"

A tingling sensation rose through Hannah's body and her hair lifted on a sudden wind. She raised her hands toward the heavens and the power of the goddess filled her. Light burst from her palms and pierced clouds and night sky.

And then she was lying flat on her back, naked, on a hard stone surface. Her arms and legs were securely tied, and her wrists and ankles were bleeding from where the straps sliced into her flesh as she had struggled. A dark form rose above her and the glint of a steely knife

146

caught her eye. Her body went rigid with fear and she screamed as the knife stabbed down toward her heart.

Before blade met flesh, she found herself standing beside the altar. Only this time Zin was strapped to it – and the blade was buried to its hilt in his chest.

Hannah screamed "*No!*" as she woke from her nightmare. Terror for Zin roared through her like a glacier rumbling over ice and rock. She knew he was in danger, knew it with everything in her heart and soul.

But in the next moment, excruciating pain ripped through her body. She screamed again and thrashed on the bed as she jerked and spasmed with every burst of agony. She went hot then cold, cold, cold. Every inch of her was in such misery that she couldn't stop screaming. Inside she felt as if she was expanding, changing, nearly bursting from her skin. Sweat broke out over her flesh and she felt as if her body was going to splinter into countless pieces.

Vaguely she heard Patricia's soothing voice, felt a hand gripping her wrist. "You'll be all right, *mi hija*. The transformation process will be over soon."

Transformation? Barely had the word registered when fresh pain spiked through her and she screamed again.

For a time, Hannah knew nothing.

When she woke again, the pain had subsided. Hannah lay panting on the bed. She was tangled in the sheet, her body sweaty, yet cold inside.

She blinked and Patricia's face came into focus. "Drink," the housekeeper said as she lifted a glass of red fluid to Hannah's lips.

Horror filled her and she started to say no, but Patricia took the opportunity to pour some into Hannah's mouth. She nearly choked as the fluid rolled over her tongue. It was disgusting, yet there was something in it that she needed and she craved. The coppery taste, the depth of the mixture.

The blood.

Hannah recoiled and the drink spilled onto the sheet covering her breasts. She stared at Patricia, unable to believe what was happing to her.

The transformation process will be over soon.

"That son of a bitch made me into a vampire." Angry tears rose up in Hannah's eyes. She could barely hold them back. "I trusted him and he turned me."

Patricia sighed. "I don't think it was intentional, but it is done nonetheless."

"Bullshit." Hannah jerked herself upright and wound the sheet tighter around her. "The bastard knew exactly what he was doing." Fire filled her head as she glanced around the room and through the doorway. "Where the hell is he? I'm going to kill him."

Patricia's mouth screwed up into a tight frown, as if something was bothering her. "He left not long ago. I think he needed to feed. Likely, he gave you too much of his own blood to be sure you survived."

"Screw him. Leaving me here to go suck some necks." The enormity of what he'd done hit her full force. "Shit." She buried her face in her hands and her words came out muffled as she spoke. "I'm going to have to live on blood? I just can't believe this. Goddamnit. I *trusted* him!"

She squeezed her eyes tight, trying to block out the pain of his betrayal. But then images came back to her from her dream, one after another until she saw Zin on an altar, a knife buried in his chest.

Her head shot up and she cut her gaze to Patricia. "Zin's in danger. I think he's gone off to do something stupid. Like battle the *Lopos* on his own. Why would he do that?"

"*Dios mio!*" Patricia reached forward and grabbed Hannah's right hand. Before Hannah could think to react, she turned the hand over and inspected Hannah's fingertips.

The blister was huge now, covering the entire end of Hannah's finger.

"How could I have missed that? Why didn't we look?" Patricia dropped Hannah's hand. "No. Oh, no!"

The housekeeper turned on her heel and rushed toward the bedroom door. "Trouble, trouble, trouble!"

Hannah scrambled from the bed. Her body was so weak she nearly tripped over the sheet. "Wait for me! And what's so freaky about my finger? Damn. Look at the time. I should have called Britt hours ago. I can call her now, right? Vampires can use phones."

"Dress first," Patricia called from down the hall, her voice edged with her own fear. "And drink a bit more of the blood-martini mix in the fridge. You'll need it to put off the blood lust and your first real feeding. I'm going to Ops to summon Creed."

"Creed, yes. Of course. Just what we need. More vampires." Hannah could barely walk, but she hurried to the bureau where she had stashed the jeans Zin had bought for her in the village just days ago. As quickly as she could, she yanked on the jeans, a T-shirt, and her socks and running shoes. All the while her mind raced over her dream and the feeling that something terrible was going to happen. She pushed thoughts of his betrayal to the back of her mind. What was important now was saving his life.

Then she'd kill him.

Hannah stumbled through the house to the kitchen and choked down an entire glass of Patricia's blood-brew. It tasted awful and wonderful at the same time, but most importantly, it relieved her strong urge to grab Patricia and bite into the poor woman's arteries.

More clearheaded after the blood fix, Hannah headed into Zin's high-tech Ops room, where she knew she'd find Patricia. Even as she hurried the best she could, she could feel more changes taking place in her body. Changes that were frightening, yet somehow exhilarating. She was starting to feel invincible, even more so than when she had blue light sprouting from her hands.

With every move she made, her steps became more powerful, more confident. Her head cleared and her senses heightened. And she *knew* things. Stuff she couldn't know. Like why the blister on her finger was important. She remembered vividly signing that book with her blood.

The Book of Blood. Her mind seemed to be downloading data, letting her understand how that bound her to the *Lopos* monsters and put her at risk.

Damn Zin. He was being noble—but so stupid!

Before she reached Ops, she could hear Patricia muttering under her breath, "Damn vampires. Can't find one when you need one. What are these weird blips on the screen? Three of them, close—ah, who the hell knows. Creed, where are you?"

Hannah reached the doorway and saw Patricia with her fingertips to her forehead. "You've got me to help you," Hannah said.

That's right, baby." Patricia gave her a quick hug and then smiled at her. "We'll have to work together to get him back. If we don't get to Hotel Rojo quick—well, I don't want to think."

"I don't know how to do the flying thing, so we'd better take the Ferrari," Hannah replied, even as she was heading for the garage.

"They could kill us, you know." Patricia ran along beside her. "They probably will kill us."

Before Hannah could answer, the doorbell rang and both Patricia and Hannah came to an abrupt stop. The housekeeper frowned. "How the hell did anyone get past the warding and without tripping the sensors?"

Hannah ran down the hall, hoping it was one of Zin's vampire friends. She flung the door open and then her jaw dropped.

Her sister Nicki and their mother stood on the doorstep, their expressions fierce and their hair blowing wildly in the wind.

And they each held a gun, pointed at Hannah.

Chapter Twelve
Deep of the Night

Zin gripped the precious piece of sheet he had taken from beneath Hannah, heart aching as he scented her delicious musk one more time. Then his nostrils flared as he took in the true scent of Hotel Rojo, which loomed before him like the gates of Hell. The red glow the *Lopos* used to snare and mesmerize unwary travelers—shining full force and shimmering in the spring chill.

Damn, but the place reeked of stale blood and rotting flesh. His lips curled back, baring his fangs. Excrement and piss and misery. Enough to gag a demon—and here at the Solstice, it was worse. How many innocents had the bastards already captured? How many hapless fools had already signed the Book of Blood?

He shifted under the cover of stones, rock, and tumbleweed, watching the weakest spot in the wards around the compound. He cut his gaze to the desert stars. In two hours, all five of the western covens would arrive to storm the *Lopos* fortress—it happened every year, and they rarely made much headway. Still, they kept trying. No doubt they saved a few humans each year, just keeping the bastards distracted.

Earlier Creed would have been organizing the troops at his own headquarters in Mexico City, no doubt wondering where the hell Zin was. *Our annual Battle of the Fangs*, he'd joke. *The Lopos at their strongest and yet their most distracted moment.*

Summer Solstice. Nothing would be different this year. Nothing except Zin.

"I'm here, old friend," he said to Creed, as if his maker lay in camouflage beside him. "I'm gonna tenderize the meat. I might not accomplish much, but I think you'll find the going a little easier."

Foolish. Suicidal. Impulsive.

Whatever.

If he didn't act now, Hannah might be killed before the covens could attack. No doubt existed in his mind that the *Lopos* would be out in full force to find her. They wouldn't have been able to sense her before, but now — well, he'd made her as obvious as a beacon.

Damn, damn, damn!

The strains of an old religious song pounded in his mind. *La Encomendación Del Alma* — the Entrustment of the Soul. It was about trusting God with the eternal essence, but Zin wasn't ready to leave the task up to a higher power just yet. First, he intended to do his part.

A strange electricity hung in the desert air. Earth energy. Energy from covens, *Vampiro*, Wiccan, and Pagan alike. Positive energy and negative energy.

And something else.

Zin couldn't quite put his finger on the difference, and he wondered if the subtle change was only in his mind.

Maybe it's just my love for Hannah. Maybe it's just that I don't care what happens to me this time. The Book — that's all that matters. Soon, they'll open it and —

Almost on cue, five *Lopos* thugs drifted out of the front door, sniffing and growling as they headed to the soft spot in the warding. With a few snarls, gnashing gore-covered fangs, they burst through, then sealed the wards behind them. Immediately, they started sniffing.

"Five. Shit." Zin held back his own snarls and instead gave the piece of sheet a little shake. So what if there were five. He could take them. He had to.

The lead *Lopos*, no flunky, easily a captain in rank — or higher — had been about to shift into his animal form. He hesitated mid-change. Zin saw his features ripple and pulse as he settled back to a man, though misshapen and bestial. The bastard's head had more lumps than a rotten seed potato.

Growling low in his throat, Zin shook the piece of sheet again. "Come on. Take it. That's it. Take it."

"She's close," the *Lopos* said in his gravelly, inhuman voice. Zin heard the surprise. "And so, so strong. Smell her, boys? She's right around here!"

The other four monsters gave an arrogant laugh and started sniffing. One at a time, they turned toward the debris hiding Zin.

"This way," said the captain.

Zin kept his fangs bared and ready. He dropped the sheet and doubled his grip on his long-sword. The AK-47 felt heavy in his left hand. The toe of his boot hovered above the detonator for four shallow land mines.

A little closer. Just a few more steps...

"Come to us, little falcon," the lead monster whispered in his best mesmerizing tone. "You can't escape a second time."

The guy was good. Zin actually felt a little tug in his own chest. He cocked an eyebrow, thinking that the asshole was damn sure of himself, that he wouldn't be expecting to find himself headless any time soon.

Inch by inch, the *Lopos* squad moved into his minefield. Zin let them take three more steps, then stomped the detonator.

The charges exploded. Sand and dust and rocks swirled up in a mighty *whump-whump-whump-whump*. A hairy arm flew past Zin's head as he stood and started firing.

Two of the bastards had been blown apart by the mines. One was hurt, but still charging toward him. Zin fired the AK-47 in a wide arc, using the force of his shots to sever the beast's head. That left the captain and one hench-dick.

"Two," Zin growled. "Better odds." He put a smaller blade in his teeth and charged out from the brush, his long-sword still gripped in one hand. Before him, the Hotel Rojo shimmered in its menacing fashion, lighting the desert with a deadly reddish glow. The long drive leading into its maw was blessedly empty.

Let it stay that way, Zin thought. *No more victims tonight.*

Between Zin and the hotel, the remaining *Lopos* changed, one to a demented-looking wolf and the other to a buzzard—with teeth. Zin fired without ceasing as the bird soared up, then plummeted toward him, talons-first.

Pain seared his shoulder as the long, fetid nails sank into his flesh. Keeping up a steady line of fire to discourage the captain, Zin hacked at the bird with the sword. He swung his head to slice it with the knife in his teeth. Images of Hannah stayed firmly forward in his mind as he fought.

In seconds, the vulture collapsed and changed back into a beast even as the captain lunged, growling, at Zin's throat. He dropped to one knee and the wolf passed over his head. He took the few moments' advantage to hack off the head of the injured *Lopos* bird-thing.

"Bastard's made of gristle," Zin grumbled.

"Impressive," said the captain, who was human-like again. Bullet wounds oozed on his chest, but as Zin watched, the bullets fell on the desert floor and the holes began to seal. "Are you alone, *Vampiro?* What kind of fool would attack us alone?"

Zin didn't answer. Talking to a *Lopos* opened the door for mesmerizing. Instead, he dropped the AK-47, took the knife out of his teeth, and began a slow, circling dance with the captain, long-sword in one hand, knife in the other. He didn't want to kill the asshole—not yet. Not until he'd been useful. Zin knew the creatures inside wouldn't come help their companion. The *Lopos* were safe with victims to slaughter, enjoying the heat and hum of the Solstice. To those animals, everyone was expendable. Maybe a few hours from now, when the squad hadn't returned, they'd quit killing and gorging and dancing and fucking long enough to see what had become of the hunt for Hannah.

Obviously, they wanted her, and not just because she had signed the Book of Blood. Because she was strong. Because her heart would nourish them.

Over my dead body. Zin rumbled and snapped his fangs together, keeping his eyes trained on the captain.

The bastard kept talking, but Zin tuned him out. He focused on the position of the captain's legs and feet, the movement of his arms, and the cast of his eyes.

Any second now…

The captain blinked once, then charged, spinning neatly to avoid one of Zin's blades. The long-sword caught the asshole once on the top of his shoulder, but not before he clawed Zin hard across the chest.

Immediately, the beast's poison roared through Zin's veins, slowing his heart, impairing his reflexes. He squinted, breathing hard, but keeping his blades aloft.

The captain retreated, nursing the wound near his neck. "Close. And the blade—it's been treated, yes? I cannot heal this scratch in the normal ways."

Fuck you, Zin thought dizzily, fighting the effects of the *Lopos* poison. *Come a little closer and let's see if you can heal a decapitation.*

The captain could clearly see his deadly venom taking effect. "Are you feeling tired, *Vampiro*?" He sauntered closer to Zin, who drew upon years of battle training to hold himself on his feet. "Why don't you fall? I'll make it quick. I promise."

Zin felt his heart gallop, and knew the bastard was already reaching for it mentally. He warded and shielded his thoughts, thrusting away the captain's influence.

The *Lopos* jerked his head as if he'd been slapped. "Well. Again, I'm impressed. But that little trick must have taken all of your energy. Fall, *Vampiro*. Fall!"

The captain inched forward, one step, then two. Zin let him come. He could hardly stop him now. The bastard's laugh echoed across the empty desert.

Dimly, Zin registered the headlights of a car heading down the drive toward Hotel Rojo. His heightened vision could make out a dark-headed, tanned woman at the wheel. She didn't seem mesmerized at all. Just...pissed off, big time.

Damn. He shook is head. *How's that for wishful thinking? Of course she's mesmerized. Of course she's a new victim. Fucking assholes. It ends tonight, damn it!*

"Fall!" commanded the *Lopos* captain, and Zin obliged. He dropped his long-sword and pitched forward, directly into the asshole's outstretched arms.

Before the *Lopos* could get a good grip, Zin stumbled sideways, grabbed the captain's forearm and pivoted until he stood behind the bastard. With no hesitation, he sank his blade into the beast's back and cut, hard and deep, in a forceful circle.

The *Lopos* let out a shriek that might have shattered windows five miles away. He tried to escape Zin's grip, to move at all, but Zin had him tight. The poison made his head pound, but he could still move much better than he let on when the captain was approaching.

"I'm an old dog," he growled into the bastard's ear as he plunged his hand into the beast's back, fumbled for a second, then wrapped his fingers around the tiny, throbbing, wriggling heart. "Hard to teach me new tricks."

Gasping and twitching, the *Lopos* stood very still, awaiting death. "Kill me then," he begged. "Do not torture me."

"Sorry. Not so easy." Zin marched the bastard around the fight's perimeter, sheathing his long-sword, picking up his AK-47 and hanging it from his belt. He glanced over his captive's shoulder and saw the dark-skinned victim heading toward the door. He gave the captain's heart a little squeeze, and the *Lopos* sagged back against him. "I need to get in that damn hotel. Get me through the door behind that woman, and I'll make it fast for you. Otherwise, well, I'll take a piece or two and leave you here for my companions to find."

Without question or hesitation, the captain took a shaky step toward Hotel Rojo, with Zin behind him, a skilled puppet-master, literally pulling the strings.

* * * * *

"Do you think you could point those things in another direction?" Hannah eyed her mother and sister and their well-aimed pistols, stunned. Her mom looked alert, focused — not confused at all. The air around her shivered and shimmered in Hannah's newly-enhanced visual field. Gone was the confused old woman. This was Elena Cordova, the woman Hannah remembered from childhood. This was the strong and vibrant single parent who'd raised Hannah and Nicki with a firm hand and warm embrace, the woman who'd worked double shifts and sometimes around the clock to make sure her girls had what they needed.

Nicki, on the other hand, was still just Nicki, and man did she ever look pissed. "What the hell's been going on? Why have you been staying here? And what's with you, Hannah? You look pale."

Hannah swallowed, feeling her fangs extend, then retract of their own volition. She was painfully aware that the change hadn't finished yet, that anything might happen in the next few hours.

I'm a vampire. Oh, my god. A vampire! What am I supposed to say to them?

"Are you going to bite us?" Elena Cordova's voice rang out clear and even. "Because if you're going to bite us, I'm going to shoot you, daughter or no."

Nicki snorted. "Bite us? Mom. Get real."

"She's a vampire. I can see it. Can't you?" Elena blinked, and tears squeezed from her eyes. "What happened, sweetheart?"

"There are worse things than becoming *Vampiro*," said a rich male voice from behind Nicki and Elena. Creed strode into view, wearing formal attire with a matching cape, just like vamps in horror flicks. His long, blond hair fell loose about his shoulders, and his golden eyes focused exclusively on Nicki's back. Hannah saw the bulge of multiple weapons beneath his tuxedo.

Silk, single-breasted, long coat, Hannah's sharpened vision informed her. She was amazed at how bright the night seemed, how it teemed with silver and gold flecks. The glittering air whirled like a halo around Creed. *Black gloves, white trim, red rose on the lapel. What is he, late for the opera?*

Nicki whirled around and almost choked at the sight of Creed in his classic suit. Elena turned around as well, and Creed quickly found himself on the business end of two guns. He didn't seem concerned. In fact, he seemed a bit amused, except for the tense look of worry on his chiseled-stone brow. He surveyed Nicki and Elena, then offered a courtly bow.

Hannah's burgeoning senses stirred. She detected shifts in the wind. Scents of animals, men, women—newcomers—five, then ten, now twenty, dropping quietly out of the sky.

"The western covens," she muttered even as they made tentative psychic contact with her to introduce themselves.

"It's raining vampires," Nicki whispered so loudly everyone could hear. "Vampires with guns and swords."

"*Vampiros*," Creed corrected. He stepped forward so fast no one had a chance to move, clasped Nicki's hand, and lifted it to his mouth. Without blinking his eerie yellow eyes, he ran his lips across her knuckles.

Hannah was surprised to note that for once in her life, Nickilyn Cordova was absolutely speechless. She jerked her hand away from Creed like he'd set her on fire instead of kissing her.

To Elena, Creed said, "My lady. You grace us with your presence."

Elena lowered her gun. For a moment, Hannah saw a flash of blue-silver above her mother. Hannah blinked and shielded her eyes, and that fast, it was gone. Her head was starting to throb, and she kept hooking her bottom lip with her fangs.

"Don't talk to my mother," Nicki instructed, recovering herself. "You people mesmerize before you bite. I've got a doctorate in psychology with a specialty in parapsychology. I'm not an idiot."

"I would never presume such a thing." Creed's normally serious voice held a note of humor. "And I was not speaking to Elena, the forward vessel. I speak to her soul, to the eldest daughter of Omecihuatl, she of two faces. Without the daughters of the creator-destroyer, we will all die this night."

Hannah bit herself again, this time from surprise. She tasted the copper of her own blood, and for a moment, her head spun. She grabbed the door facing behind her mother and sister.

"Mother of God," Creed murmured, at last turning his attention to Hannah. "I didn't believe it when I first sensed it. The bastard turned you! Tonight, of all nights. How are you even walking?"

"I don't know," Hannah grumbled, running her tongue over the healing holes in her lip. "But we need to go save Zin so I can kill him, okay?"

And with that, she fainted into her mother's arms.

The sky...a bright darkness never seen before. The stars — they burned like torches, hurting her eyes, splintering her mind. Below her, the desert flamed and flickered. The world seemed to be on fire.

"Fly," urged a voice that was familiar, but not desired. She didn't want this voice. She wanted the other one, the one that spoke to her heart.

"Zin," Hannah whispered. "Zin."

She woke suddenly, feeling the sting of wind against her face.

"She's coming around," Nicki said from somewhere on Mars, only it wasn't Mars. Her voice came from the front seat of her vintage Bentley Continental. Nicki had a thing about fancy cars. Good thing she made a fortune on the stock market, investing Hannah's profits for the both of them and their mother.

Hannah tried to unravel the sock smothering her brain, but it was hard.

Was Creed driving a car?

The idea seemed ludicrous. Creed was such a...not car...man. *Vampire*, Hannah reminded herself. *Ancient, bloodsucking fiend. Like me. Well, without the ancient part.*

"Damn," she mumbled, massaging her temples. She could use one of Patricia's concoctions right about now. "Where's Patricia?" she tried to ask, but what came out was, "Mmmgpphtthllggffft."

Someone patted her shoulder. Her mom. Her mom with the clear, focused eyes. "Stay calm, honey. We're on our way to Hotel Rojo."

"Creed, the nice gentleman driving the roadster and eying your sister, says we're going to save your Eternal Mate and murder a bunch of monsters called *Lopos*. If you look out your window — well, there are dozens of *Vampiros* running and flying along side." Elena leaned close and kissed her on the cheek. "Some of them have guns. I'm a little worried."

Hannah wanted to vomit. The stars felt too bright. Her bottom lip was full of holes. The night seemed to hold a thousand scents, each more fascinating and overwhelming than the one before. One smell, however, was more than familiar and growing stronger by the second. An earthy, basic, male musk she'd recognize anywhere.

Zin. Eternal Mate. Yes, that's exactly what he was.

Her fangs extended and retracted, extended and retracted. Hannah tried to sit up. Her lover's scent mingled with fetid, rotten dirt. The smell of gore and graves. She growled, feeling a surge of strength and power. *Lopos.* She'd kill them all, especially if they hurt Zin.

"I don't understand this Daughters of Omecihuatl thing," Nicki was saying. "But two days ago, mom just...snapped out of her confusion. After she burned the nursing home down. Thank God nobody was hurt. It was weird, though. All the staff and all the patients had gone out into the desert for a cookout instead of being in the home when it got torched, everyone but Mom. What's going on with that?"

"We don't have all the answers," Creed admitted in his smooth yet genuine fashion. "But we've been waiting for centuries. I know your mother is of the line—from visions, and from her energy signature. You should have seen her on the monitors. You and Hannah, too."

There was a pause, and then Nicki, sounding tense and angry. "Why did this Zin bastard make my sister a *Vampiro?*"

"I don't have the answer to that either, but Patricia said it was an accident."

"And you trust Patricia?"

Classic Nicki. Always wary. Hannah squinted, trying to see the outline of her sister's face in the bright of the night. Her vision was still blurred, but she could tell Nicki was frowning.

"I would put my life in her hands." Creed managed to sound emphatic, which seemed out of character for him. "It galled her to be left behind, but there was no choice. I wouldn't expose her to the carnage we're about to face. She...couldn't bear to watch the killing."

"So, Zin does this horrid thing by accident, then runs off into the night and strands Hannah with the change alone?" Nicki sniffed at the end of her sentence. Hannah heard a clack-clack sound afterward, and knew her sister was tapping her sculpted nails against the dashboard.

"It's not so horrid as all that, *mi alma*." Creed's tone was still serious. "We *Vampiros* have our good points."

"Whatever," Nicki snapped.

"He didn't expect her to be awake so soon. New-mades usually take a few days to fully rouse. I'm sure Zin thought Patricia could handle it, and that Patricia would call me to help if he failed to come back."

Another pause, and, "So, if Zin's dead, will you help Hannah?"

Hannah tensed, feeling sicker than ever.

"Absolutely. And I'll protect her even to my dying breath. Just as I will protect your mother—and you."

"I don't need your protection."

"From your lips to Omecihuatl's ears." Creed took a slow breath as the reddish glow of Hotel Rojo caused Hannah to sit straight up in her seat, heart hammering. Sharp pains stabbed through her blistered finger, and she briefly considered biting it off.

Zin! Her chest ached even more fiercely. *Please, please, be okay.*

Chapter Thirteen
Summer Solstice

Zin had never made it inside the *Lopos* lair before, at least not past the front steps. He'd never been desperate enough to die for his goal.

Maybe that was the problem. He blinked. Blood-sweat covered his forehead, and the *Lopos* poison worked on his strength. No way was he giving up. He'd fight to the last breath and step. *See, if we were all suicidal, if we all had Eternal Mates to protect – damned if this whole fight wouldn't be over before it started.*

"Coatlicue, I'm coming for you." He gnashed his fangs once, then continued, speaking at a volume that only he could hear. "Finally, after all these years, I'll get you and Huitzilopochtli, too. This time, you're mine."

The bowels of the *Lopos* lair stank like sewage. Zin barely choked in a breath as he marched the captain forward into Hotel Rojo, behind the dark, beautiful woman who had pulled up the drive during the fight. Another traveler straggled in behind them—this one a man with a scruffy brown beard and a swaggering, self-important air. Zin thought it odd that he hadn't seen the man's car approach. He wondered if the guy had had his lights off when he came down the drive.

Neither the woman nor the white-suited, pompous ass noticed Zin or Zin's half-dead captive, because Zin willed them not to see. He managed to slip them behind some greenery as a flunky lumbered out to meet the two new guests—and he realized his talents with mental persuasion hadn't been needed at all. The two visitors were mesmerized by *Lopos* spells, big time. They didn't notice that the "hotel employee" looked like a cross between a jackal and a zombie. A seven-foot tall zombie with green, rotting cheeks.

Zin shifted his captive, keeping a firm grip on the bastard's heart. "Don't move," he hissed quietly. "Keep us unseen."

The captain nodded. Zin waited for the flunky to take out the Book of Blood — but he didn't.

Damn!

"Right this way," the bastard said, silk-voiced, like a waiter in some five-star restaurant. "You're just in time for the festivities."

As the new guests and the jackal-beast drifted off down the hallway, Zin swore under his breath. He frog-marched the captain over to the counter and made a quick, mad search for the Book.

It wasn't there.

"Shit! Where is it?" he asked himself more than anything, but the captain started to laugh.

"Kill me now, you *Vampiro* desert mouse. You'll never get into the temple — and even if you did, they're all there. Everyone. And you're all alone, suffering from our fine poison, growing weaker by the second."

Zin seethed. A few minutes earlier, and he might have reached the Book.

And I might have run right into twenty or so Lopos — *before they got blood-drunk on sacrifices.*

"Come on," he growled to his captive, mustering the strength still at his command. "To the temple."

"My pleasure," said the beast, still laughing. "At least I might watch you die."

Together, they moved down stone hallways and around blind corners. Zin didn't care about caution any more. He didn't care about anything.

Time was running out. He could feel it. If he didn't find that fucking Book soon, he'd die from the poison. Worse yet, the

Lopos would use the Book of Blood to summon Hannah—or find her to drag her back to the temple. Gods. She was probably still unconscious. She'd have no chance—and Patricia, they'd kill her, too, for sport. Or worse. They might drag her to this forsaken house of horrors and make her serve alongside her twisted children.

"Not gonna happen." He shoved his captive ahead of him, careful to keep hold of his heart. They lurched into a large, empty courtyard open to the sky. Zin glanced up, but instantly wished he hadn't. The stars above his head blurred in and out, obscured by the powerful, poisonous *Lopos* wards.

His captive started to drop their shielding, but Zin tightened his grip on the bastard's heart. "You know your only hope is to get me in the temple—and it's a little hope, at that."

They staggered together toward cacti and stone monuments crouched around them. Torches burned low and faint on tall poles, casting shadows and horrible orange flickers across the stones.

Just like before, Zin thought. He felt sick, but more than that, he felt furious. *Got it all planned, don't you Coatlicue? You think we're singing the same song, second verse. Well, got news for you, you perverted bitch. This time, I'm here* first.

Driven more by rage and determination than actual strength, Zin forced his captive up several steps, to the top level of what had to be the temple. It had to be. Just like it was all those centuries ago.

A large chamber loomed ahead, and to the right of the chamber door, the *chacmool* waiting for the bloody hearts of *Lopos* victims. Ceremonial torches burned in a perfect circle around the *chacmool*.

"Ready. It's all ready." Zin fought to keep his thoughts clear even as the poison fought to muddle his brain. "That means they're all inside, at the altar."

The captain sniggered.

Biting back a roar of frustration, half-mad from the effects of the claw-venom, Zin shoved the beast through the chamber door, barely keeping his hand in the bastard's back. Barely keeping hold of that all-important heart.

Just as he expected, a full cadre of *Lopos* in full ceremonial dress huddled around a table. A woman's voice chanted in the old language, speaking words that tore at Zin's memory and mind.

Was that Aki on the table? Was it Hannah?

No!

Did he say that to himself, or roar it aloud?

Zin couldn't tell any longer. The chanting stopped abruptly, which was answer enough.

He heard someone shout, "Hold! Leave him be. Just bar the doors."

The sound of wood thunking against stone nearly split open Zin's throbbing head. His grip on the captain's heart faltered, but he managed to keep it—even as more thunks battered his senses. These were wood-on-wood, no doubt heavy bars falling into place to secure the temple doors until the sacrifices were completed.

"Hello, old friend," came the voice again.

His vision narrowed to just one view. A woman with countless braids and curls twisted above her head, emeralds and precious gems woven through the black locks. Zin would have known that haughty stance, recognized those overdone, gilded robes anywhere—and those soulless black-pit eyes.

"Coatlicue," he said coldly, suddenly aware that she had gone silent. The "goddess" of old, the murderer who took the first incarnation of his Eternal Mate from him, was staring at him with a faint smile on her thick, bloody lips. "I was never your friend. And to prove it, I'm going to kill you, you ugly, warped bitch from hell."

Zin could see through the glamour then. He blinked, the vision swimming in his mind. Skull at her waist, robe of hissing serpents. And on the altar below her, she had her first victim, a naked man—the arrogant idiot who had strolled in behind Zin and the captain. Poor asshole didn't even seem to know he was still in the world, much less tied to a stone table under the merciless hands of a cannibalistic monster.

The other potential sacrifices milled in a small group to the left, well-controlled by three young boys who looked so, so sadly like Patricia. Zin's poison-soaked thoughts registered their sad, empty eyes. Blood servants, neither with soul, nor without.

Coatlicue raised her ceremonial dagger high. The dagger she had once used to kill Aki.

"We'll see who comes out of this alive," she said lightly, and plunged the blade home. In two quick moves, she had the poor man's heart. He was dead before Zin could make his muscles obey his command to move.

Without conscious thought, he released his hold on the captain and shoved him hard into the group of *Lopos* around the altar. Immediately, the beast ripped the head off his nearest companion and greedily fed on the blood to begin his own restoration.

The world moved in slow motion to Zin's fevered brain. He staggered forward, drawing his sword, pulling out the AK-47, shooting in wild arcs, barely able to keep the bullets away from the innocents on the left.

Coatlicue seemed unconcerned by his advance, or the loyal subjects dropping before him. Because she had commanded them to leave him alone, they did so. Only her son, Huitzilopochtli, seemed a little nervous. The powerful looking bastard stood beside the bitch that sired him.

With an almost graceful flick of the wrist, Coatlicue released the dead man's bonds and shoved his body off the altar, into the waiting arms—and jaws of her faithful acolytes. The ones who were still standing, anyway.

Zin barely registered what was happening as the beasts fell on the corpse. He had eyes only for Coatlicue and Huitzilopochtli.

"Where's the Book?" he croaked, beheading the captain, who was stupid enough to take him on a second time. Zin squeezed off a few rounds from the AK-47, but dropped it a second later. The strength in his hands was failing. The poison, the wards—everything weighed too heavy now. He still had his long-sword, though. And the determination of a man who would not let his woman fall victim to these monsters a second time.

Clutching the sword in both fists, Zin staggered the last few steps. There was nothing between them now except the blood-soaked stone table. In his increasing stupor, Zin thought he saw the table drinking the spillage.

The false *Mexica* goddess grinned at him. Her gore-soaked teeth gleamed red and black in the torch light.

"The Book," he said, battling to keep his grip on the sword.

"Get it," Coatlicue told her son.

Huitzilopochtli quickly complied.

Why are they doing this? Zin wondered dimly. *They could take me, easy.*

Coatlicue took the Book of Blood from her son and placed it on the stone table. Carefully, delicately, she turned the pages. The serpents on her gown hissed and squirmed, as if their excitement was growing along with hers.

"Is this what you want, Zin of the True People?" She ran her gnarled, filth-encrusted finger down a list of red-scrawled names. "You want to tear out a page? Mayhap destroy a bargain made in good faith, of free will?"

Zin lunged forward, swinging his sword.

"Hold him," Coatlicue said with chilly precision.

She stepped back as what felt like a hundred hands grabbed Zin. In the blink of an eye, his sword was gone. His clothes were gone. The *Lopos* he had failed to kill were forcing him down to the table, and he couldn't fight them.

Despair ripped at his very essence. He tried to resist, not for his life, not for his safety, but for Hannah. For Patricia. For the unsuspecting mesmerized fools standing against the temple wall.

"Get the woman," Coatlicue hissed to her demented offspring. "The dark one—Britt. She's important to the one we seek. Tie her down with this one."

Zin's thoughts rose and fell like a stormy sea. They were going to use his blood and the woman's to nourish the Book, to summon Hannah against her will.

She's using me to kill my love. Again.

"No," he said with almost no volume, fighting against his bonds in between racking tremors induced by the poison.

The woman, Britt, even kicked and fussed a little, which was amazing, considering her mesmerized state. Zin couldn't quite process all she said, but he caught, "No wonder she didn't call," "you crazy vampire bastards," and "asshole don't touch me if you want to keep your dick."

All to no avail. The fiery creature was soon lashed beside him, crowding into his shoulder, swearing under her breath.

Coatlicue opened the Book of Blood and laid it across Britt's chest and Zin's, too. She raised her bloody dagger and started a new chant, drawing on old, sinister magic to bring Hannah's energy to her, willing or not.

Why do they want her so badly? Just to kill me? It didn't seem logical to Zin, but then, nothing seemed logical to him any longer. After all his centuries of existence, he was going to die still understanding so very little about life and its many mysteries.

Sooner than he thought possible, Coatlicue finished her spell and handed her damned dagger to her son.

"You may do the honors. The gods will favor you with strength."

The beast-man nodded.

Zin squinted at the dagger, waiting for it to plunge down into the pages, all the way through to his heart. The bastard would stab the woman next, strengthening the call. And Zin could do nothing. Not a damned thing.

"Come to me, daughter of Omecihuatl," the false god commanded — and to Zin's dulled senses, the room exploded and Huitzilopochtli seemed to come apart at the seams.

Blue light burst from his eyes, his mouth, his nose, and openings no human — nor beast — should have. The dagger in his hand trembled, then fell harmless atop the Book of Blood. Then, quick as that, he disappeared. No ashes, no flash of light, no nothing — he was just gone. Coatlicue roared with rage, swiping a hand through the space where her son once stood.

"Deserter!" she shrieked. "Come back. Come back!"

The light began to overwhelm Zin, along with the *Lopos* poison. The last thing he heard before he faced the darkness of death was three steady, cool female voices saying, "No need to call the daughters of Omecihuatl. We're already here."

Hannah stood arm in arm with her mother and sister, wearing a pair of Nicki's kick-ass Raybans. For the moment, her fangs were bared, and her bottom lip had no fresh holes. Blue fire surrounded the three women like an impenetrable curtain — just like Creed thought it would if they concentrated their emotions and worked together. They found themselves directly behind the spot Huitzilopochtli had stood, and directly in the center of the hole they had just blasted in the temple wall with the help of the *Vampiros*.

Countless *Vampiros* who were, even as she processed the scene before her, streaming into the *Lopos* lair, wielding sword, knife, gun, and claw against their enemies.

"Good show," said Creed as he stalked into the temple. "Now get out. Your power is fading already. Hannah's too weak to keep this up — and this is no place for new-mades or humans."

At once, Nicki and Elena started to withdraw from the Hotel Rojo. Hannah shook loose of them and she ran forward instead, shrieking like a bird of prey as she saw the two bloody, weak figures on the sacrificial table. Zin—and, damn it all to hell—Britt, too!

Frantically, Hannah tugged at their bonds, ripping one after the other. Her head spun. She felt weak enough to die on the spot, but no way was she going down now. Britt was blinking like crazy and screaming, obviously no longer mesmerized. Zin, however, was still as death. Had the beasts sacrificed him already? Had they taken his heart?

Hannah was vaguely aware of long nails digging into her shoulder, but she ignored those, too. All she cared about was releasing Britt and Zin.

Britt was alert enough to help as the *Vampiro-Lopos* battle raged. Hannah had no idea who was winning. She almost didn't care.

"Zin!" The force of her voice surprised her. "Wake up, Zin!"

And then the claws in her arms dug deeper. Hannah cried out and turned, doing her best to focus her emotions and call the blue light back to her.

Nothing happened, except that she staggered and fell.

Too weak to keep this up...

Creed's words haunted her as she tried to get to her feet, only to be shoved to the floor by Coatlicue herself. Hannah rolled under the stone table—and came face to face with a partially-eaten corpse she couldn't help but recognize.

"Tim?" she said, deeply shocked.

Timothy Mix, of course, couldn't answer her. His spared eye gazed upward, and his mouth was frozen in what looked like a scream of terror.

Damn. He was probably following Britt. Jeez. Oh, jeez.

She rolled back out from under the table, back to the feet of Coatlicue. The bitch looked like she was made of moving snakes. She still had the mad gleam in her eyes, the same gleam she'd had when she had sacrificed the victim on Hannah's first visit to the Hotel Rojo. She still had the dagger, too. And she was holding the Book Hannah signed in blood.

"I need your heart," Coatlicue said as if Armageddon weren't occurring in her temple. "It's your choice—his heart, or yours."

As Hannah finally managed to stand, she realized the *Vampiros* were just about tied in combat with the *Lopos*. Many fallen on both sides. A lot of growling and bloody biting and chopping and shooting. Animals shifted to beasts or *Vampiros*, then right back to animals again. And still, against the far wall, was a group of dazed-looking victims, corralled by Patricia's sons and the awful doorman-beast who'd poisoned Hannah with his claws all those days ago.

Behind her, on the sacrificial table, Zin lay without moving. Britt, still naked, was staggering across the battle zone, trying to get to the victims. She paused only to pick up a sword and swing it wildly at anything that came to close. A *Vampiro* leaped up toward the ceiling, then landed neatly beside her. He seemed to be trying to help, even though Britt was trying to kill him.

He looks like a pirate, Hannah thought. She glanced outside the hole in the temple. No sign of her mother or sister. Good. They were safe. Creed would take care of them.

"Give me your heart," Coatlicue repeated doggedly. "And I will spare him this night. Honor your bargain." She clutched the Book to her chest, and Hannah felt compelled to consent. She would have felt compelled, spell or no. She couldn't let Zin die. Far off in the distance, Hannah heard a deep, rumbling roar. She had no idea what it was, but it sounded like the end of the world.

Did it matter?

"Let me help him, and I'll do what you want." Hannah folded her arms, trying to look tougher than she felt.

Coatlicue shrugged. "Give him a little blood if you must. Maybe he'll wake in time to see me kill you—again. Ah, now that would be sweet."

Shaking, not certain of what she was doing, Hannah used her nails to slice open her own wrist. Desperately, she pressed the swelling line of blood against Zin's tight, pale lips. "Drink," she whispered, bending over him. She kissed his forehead, felt the cool pressure of his mouth on her torn flesh. From the scratches on his chest and the pale cast of his skin, she was sure he'd been poisoned, like before.

And, as before, it was bad. Worse yet, he'd taken her blood, but he still wasn't moving at all.

The rumble-roar grew louder, and Hannah felt sure it was death approaching.

I'm too late, she thought with growing dread. *Damn you. Did you have to die for me?*

"I love you," she whispered softly into his ear, keeping her wrist firm against his lips, willing her *Vampiro* blood to heal her Eternal Mate. "Don't leave me now. You've got a lot of explaining to do."

Zin still didn't move.

Grinding fang against lip, Hannah gave him a final kiss on the cheek, then stood to face Coatlicue. Grief and rage mingled to fire up the strange power in her soul, the power of her lineage to Omecihuatl.

"Lie down on the altar table beside your lover," the false goddess instructed.

Hannah felt the force of the Book's command as Coatlicue held it—felt the force, but fought it, using that power.

You killed him. I'm going to kill you. She projected that thought toward Coatlicue and hoped the bitch could hear it. "Go to hell," she said through her misbehaving fangs. The rumble-roar outside was so loud she barely heard herself.

Coatlicue's dead eyes narrowed. "You made a bargain."

Hannah shrugged and adjusted her sunglasses. "I lied."

"Get on that table!"

Once more, Hannah blinked furiously behind her sister's Raybans and used every drop of her unusual strength to fight the compulsion to comply. "Make me."

Bellowing with rage, Coatlicue lunged toward her, dagger raised.

Hannah hurled herself at Coatlicue, feeling the telltale surge of her strange power. Light blazed around them as they clashed in front of the ruined temple wall.

"Unhand me!" Coatlicue commanded, stubbornly squeezing her eyes shut against the glow.

Hannah couldn't resist any more. She fell backward against the table, glowing harsh blue—but, just like before, the light was already fading. A bright yellow light took its place.

Coatlicue whirled toward the shattered wall, holding the Book of Blood before her.

Zin's big Harley Hog came blasting through the fallen stones, spraying shards and gravel in every direction. A few pieces bounced off Hannah's sunglasses. The little figure steering it didn't seem big enough to drive the thing, much less big enough to wear such a huge helmet. That little figure shut off the bike, popped the stand, and leaped off the leather seat, at the same time unstrapping what looked like a giant leaf blower.

Hannah's jaw dropped as the leaf blower spit a line of flame straight at the Book of Blood.

Coatlicue wailed as the pages in her fingers burst into flame. The snakes on her gown rattled and hissed and started to fall to the temple floor. The Book fell to the floor too, the flames immediately dying before it burned to bits.

Hannah didn't hesitate. She hoisted herself on the sacrificial table and leaped onto Coatlicue's back before Coatlicue could retrieve the charred Book from the stone floor. "You're so going down, bitch," Hannah managed as the false goddess started beating her against a jagged stone edge of the blasted wall.

"Let-her-go!" the little motorcycle-driver shouted, trying to fire up the flamethrower again.

Immediately, Hannah knew who it was.

"Patricia! Help! Burn her. My fire's not working! Stupid— change—Zin—"

Patricia ripped off her helmet, threw it at Coatlicue, then started pounding the *Lopos* with the stubbornly silent flamethrower.

"Not again," she was saying. "Not again, not again, not again! You get your filthy claws off my family. I mean it!"

Screeching with fury, Coatlicue managed to throw Hannah over her shoulder. Hannah flapped her arms as if she could fly, or force herself to change into the bird from her visions. No such luck. She sailed over the heads of battling *Lopos* and *Vampiros*, bowling into the groggy victims clotted against the temple's far wall. Britt was there, and the pirate *Vampiro*. They both had swords raised, ready to hack into three young blood-servants, who were snarling and clawing at them, looking pained and desperate.

"Don't!" Hannah cried. She kicked out at the doorman-beast, who had been trying to stand up. He collapsed back to the floor.

At that moment, Coatlicue grabbed Patricia around the neck and lowered her deadly fangs toward Patricia's vulnerable throat. Patricia crammed the end of the flamethrower in the bitch's mouth and jammed it between the sharp, curved teeth, but Hannah knew the determined little woman couldn't hold out for long.

Another *Lopos* raised a sword over Zin, clearly intending to plunge it into his heart. Creed was trying to get to him, but two beasts were literally chewing on his ankles, holding him back.

To Hannah's horror, her mother and sister came flying back through the hole in the temple wall, herded by two drooling monsters who looked like monkey-dinosaur hybrids.

Vampiros were dropping to their knees. Coatlicue happily sucked on the dead end of the flamethrower and strangled Patricia, even as she somehow managed to stoop down to retrieve her Book.

"Stop!" Hannah screamed, with the full force of her heart and soul behind that one word. "Stop!"

She felt her body shake. Her fangs burst from their sheaths and pierced her lips yet again. Her eyes felt like hot coals behind the Raybans. She raised both hands on instinct, palm out, and the brightest light she could imagine exploded from every inch of her skin.

Images seared forever into her mind.

The Book of Blood bursting into wildfire, turning to ash in a split second...

Coatlicue tearing apart at her seams, just like her son did...

Beams of blue light coursing through Nicki and Elena, doubling in strength, stretching around the room, burning *Lopos* into piles of char, leaving humans and *Vampiros* untouched...

Zin, rising from his death-like stupor like some prince in a fairytale, so handsome, so unbelievably beautiful as he lifted above the blue light, shifted into jaguar form, and leaped toward her...

"Zin," Hannah gasped, sinking to her knees.

She couldn't see. She was blind. All around her, people sobbed and fought for breath.

Odd, but her extra senses picked up more humans than there should be, more than she had counted before.

How was that possible?

What had happened?

The detestable rotting-flesh smell of the temple cleared, along with scent of smoke. Purged. Cleansed.

All sense of the *Lopos* left Hannah. Were they all gone?

"It's your choice," someone was saying to Patricia, who was sobbing wildly.

God, did I burn up her children while she watched?

All energy, all hope flowed out of Hannah like her tears, hot and red and salty.

She pitched forward into a pair of heavily muscled arms.

"*Mi alma,*" was the last phrase she heard.

Chapter Fourteen
Dawn

Laughter, crying, exclamations of joy...everything swirled together, in and out, out and in Hannah's mind like ribbons of brilliant color and light. She felt warm, safe and secure in her drowsy state, and her own happiness mingled with the joy she heard around her.

That awful sense of powerlessness she'd had for the last year—completely gone. Alienation from her music—over. Even now, she could feel words brimming in her mind, feel notes singing through her heart. Loneliness—that was also a thing of the past. Even barely aware of her surroundings, Hannah knew everything in her life had changed, and for the better.

As her senses came alive, she felt the soreness in her body and in her lower lip. Her fangs slipped out and then retracted again as she heard the pounding of a heart beneath her ear, felt warm arms wrapped around her, surrounded by the scent of the man she loved.

Slowly she opened her eyelids and looked up to see Zin smiling down at her. She was in his lap and they were seated on the leather couch in his living room. From her peripheral vision, she saw several men and women talking animatedly, heard more exclamations, more laughter, more sounds of crying.

Zin gently brushed her hair out of her face and she brought her full attention to him. "*Mi alma*," he murmured as he leaned down to kiss her temple. "You saved us all."

He pulled away and Hannah frowned at the sudden memory. "No." Her voice cracked and she cleared her throat. "Patricia did. If she hadn't come in with that leaf-blower fire-shooter, we'd all be dead. And her sons—oh, my God. What did I do?"

"Be easy, my love." Zin kissed her forehead, then reached for a glass filled with blood-red fluid that sat on the end table. "First you need this to help regain your strength. It's an even more powerful version of Patricia's 'martinis.' Drink, then I'll answer your questions."

Hannah looked from the bloody drink to Zin and thought about arguing. But the need to feed was so intense that she nearly snatched it out of his hands. He brought it up to her mouth and she drank, allowing the supercharged mixture of herbs, blood, and tequila to flow over her tongue and down her throat.

Nasty stuff. But even as she drank it, she could feel the potion starting to work, her strength returning, and her blood lust assuaged—for the moment.

When she finished, Zin took the glass and set it aside on an end table. "That should take care of things until tomorrow."

"Now tell me what happened," Hannah demanded, half-terrified of what she would hear. "What did I do?"

"Your power is incredible—you have no idea. I didn't even know it was possible. Neither did Creed."

"What do you mean?" Hannah blinked at him, still unwilling to look around the room, still feeling sick with dread over what had become of poor Patricia's heart at the sight of all that death and destruction.

"You cleansed the Hotel Rojo." Zin trailed his finger over her lips. "When you burned the Book of Blood and destroyed Coatlicue, all the blood slaves were instantly released—including Patricia's kids."

Hannah bolted upright in Zin's lap and bumped his nose, but she ignored him as her gaze riveted on the scene before her. Patricia was crying and kissing and hugging three young men, as if she was afraid to let them go. Beside her a tall and sexy older vampire looked on with an expression of pride. Patricia turned her tear-stained face to him and planted a kiss on his lips before hugging the three young men again. Hannah's mother and sister looked on, along with Britt—who was, for once, wearing clothes.

"My babies," Patricia was saying, over and over. "Look at them! I missed you so much. I've been waiting and waiting and waiting."

Hannah felt tears well in her own eyes and a lump formed in her throat. "Her sons. Her husband. They're all right. But how?"

Zin eased to his feet at the same time he helped Hannah to hers. "Her husband was the beast doorman. You released him from servitude, but in order to save his life, Creed turned him to *Vampiro*—with Patricia's permission, of course. Others were too far gone for transfusion, and many chose to pass into the land of the dead—but Creed salvaged all that he could."

"Where is Creed?" Hannah muttered, even though she couldn't take her gaze from the scene. The three young men were handsome and healthy, nothing like the blood servants they had been in the Hotel Rojo. They had aged, filled out— clearly human. Clearly strong in their own right.

Zin's arm draped around her shoulders and she glanced up at him. "He's got the rescued *Vampiros* and the rest of the coven in the back rooms, tending everybody's wounds. William's gone out to collect—er—a few willing donors. Anyone who wasn't wounded is returning the former blood servants to their homes."

"All the blood servants were released," Hannah said quietly, marveling at how her enhanced sight and vision picked every nuance and detail. When he nodded she asked, "And what about everything else?"

The corner of his mouth curved into a grin. "*Querida*, you and your sister and your mom—you flattened the place. That blue light stuff—man, is it ever kick-ass when the three of you team up. Nothing left but ashes and a bunch of stones, and we're planning to bury all that tomorrow night."

Just then, Patricia spotted Hannah and grabbed two of her sons' hands and dragged them over to Hannah. "You brought my babies back." She released the young men long enough to hug Hannah, then put her arms back around the boys' waists. "I had given up hope and you returned them to me."

Hannah shook her head. "It was all of us. If you hadn't come when you did, we wouldn't have made it."

"Baby," Patricia said as she once more stopped holding her sons long enough to grasp Hannah's hands in hers, "you have a gift. And with that gift, you gave me back my family."

At the loving expression in Patricia's gaze, and the joy she saw there, tears trickled down Hannah's cheeks.

But the next thing she knew, Hannah was swarmed by her own family. Nicki and Britt and her mother. Hannah couldn't believe how healthy and alive her mother was, and more tears streamed down her face. She was so overcome with her own joy that she could barely speak.

Elena hugged Hannah and smiled. "I'm so proud of you. I've always been proud of you."

"I love you, Mama." Hannah couldn't stop crying. "I've missed you more than you can imagine."

Britt stepped between the two and cleared her throat. "You do anything like this disappearing-into-a-vampire's-desert-lair shit again," she said, "I'll personally kick your ass. Hell, I should anyway."

Nicki braced her hands on her hips. "Get in line."

Despite her tears, Hannah had to laugh at the seriousness of their expressions. But at the same time she realized that maybe Patricia was right, and that she did have a gift. As *Vampiro* and the daughter of Omecihuatl—whatever that meant—maybe she could help Zin get rid of more underworld scum.

At the thought of Zin, she looked over her shoulder at the tall man behind her. Even as she had celebrated with Patricia's family and her own, she had felt his constant presence.

Everything and everyone around her faded away as she looked up at her vampire. His heat radiated through her and she heard the slow pounding of his heart, the rush of blood through his veins. An animal part of her woke, and she wanted to kiss him, claw him, and bite him all at once.

"Why did you turn me?" She clenched her hands, willing them to not touch him. "I trusted you."

"I am sorry, *mi alma*." He stroked his knuckles along her jaw, never taking his gaze from hers. "I won't make excuses. I screwed up and I don't blame you for hating me."

"I don't hate you. You really pissed me off, but I don't hate you." She took a deep breath. "I'm pretty sure I love you."

For a moment Zin looked taken aback, but then a slow smile spread over his handsome face, and something sparked in his dark eyes. "I think you and I have some talking to do."

Hannah smiled. "Yeah. Talking."

Zin scooped her up into his arms and she squealed with laughter and clung to his neck. While he strode from the room and down the hall, Hannah heard catcalls and whistles behind them, along with Nicki's, "Be damn sure you take care of her," and Britt's, "Or we'll both be after your ass. I mean your heart. Or your head! Damn, I need to get a sword…"

When they reached Zin's room, the door slammed shut behind them and they were alone.

Hannah expected to feel nervous or frustrated or angry—something. But all she felt was a needy and deeply vested urge to touch the man she loved.

Zin set Hannah on her feet and settled his hands upon her waist. Before Hannah could think better of it or find a reason not to, she pushed aside his vest and placed her hands on his chest.

Yes, so right. So real.

Beneath her fingertips she felt the pounding of his heart, his slow and even breathing. Throughout the house she still sensed humans and *Vampiro* alike, but that all slipped away as she and

Zin focused on one another. Damn, but she could see him now — really *see* him in her new, enhanced vampire way.

He was even more handsome than she remembered. Classic lines, chiseled body, wisdom, grace, daring, experience, and rebellion, all rolled into one incredible male specimen.

Words to new songs lit up her mind, describing his masculine beauty, paying homage to his tenderness and devotion.

I get it now. All those love songs. Finally, I understand.

She slid her fingers up his chest to his shoulders and pushed his long black hair out of the way as she linked her arms around his neck. His dark eyes held hers, and the seriousness in his expression caused her belly to quiver.

"I love you, *mi alma.*" He raised one hand and cupped one side of her face. She leaned into the touch, loving the feel of his palm against her cheek, the strength in his hand, the strength in his very being.

"I love you." She rose up and lightly kissed the corner of his mouth. "Even if you are a big idiot for going off to fight those *Lopos* alone. You could have been killed."

He slid his hand into her hair and his lips hovered above hers. "I would do anything for you. Anything at all."

"Then promise me you'll never do something so damn foolish again." With a brush of her lips against his, she added, "Promise me. I can't lose you."

Zin knew he wouldn't hesitate to do it again, but he carefully shielded these thoughts from Hannah. He would protect his woman with everything he had, and he didn't consider that foolish at all. So it was only a small lie when he murmured, "I promise not to do anything foolish. Is that better?"

Hannah frowned and nodded. "I think so."

He kissed the frown right off her face. She tasted so sweet and so good. He'd never tasted anything so wonderful, never felt anything like he did for Hannah. She was everything to him.

The Earth, the sky, the sun, moon, and stars. She was his world. Every beat of her heart was music to him. The song of her blood in her veins made him dizzy.

A small moan escaped Hannah's lips. She slipped her tongue into his mouth and sighed. Her complete trust and giving of herself was such a gift that he could barely think past the moment.

When at last they broke the kiss, Zin raised his head and studied her golden-green eyes. "I can't get enough of you."

"Even if I'm the descendant of a goddess I barely got to study in my history classes?" Hannah stepped back and he let his hands slip away from her. She pulled her T-shirt over her head and tossed it aside.

Zin's breath caught and he watched, mesmerized, as she slowly stripped out of clothing that had been ruined in the fight with the *Lopos*. Her hair was wild about her shoulders, a smudge across one cheek, scratches on her arms, and healing wounds graced her lower lip.

"You're a goddess in your own right, *mi alma*."

Like the first time he had looked upon her, he had never seen a more beautiful sight, but now, more than ever, because this woman loved him as much as he loved her. He had heard it in her voice, and felt it in the way she kissed him, could see it in her eyes, and when he opened up his mind to her, he could hear it in her thoughts.

I love you, Zin, she was saying. *I'll always love you.*

Mi corazón, he responded as he took a step toward her, *tu esta mi amore, siempre.*

Hannah held her hand up. "Stop. Just watch me."

He clenched his hands at his sides. "I need to touch you."

She smiled. "You will. In time. We have lots of time, remember? All that stuff you kept telling me before, about patience?"

Zin wanted to groan.

With agonizing slowness, she kicked off her shoes and started to strip. He could smell her in new ways with each layer and garment she removed. He could hear the rush of her blood all the louder — mingling with his own.

She kicked off her shoes, then peeled off her jeans. When she stood only in her bra and panties, she took them off in a slow and sensuous tease.

The moment she was completely naked, Zin couldn't take it anymore. He reached out and pulled her flush against his body, and he pressed his erection tight to her belly, the jaguar ring at her navel pressing into her flesh.

Holding him in check with her newfound *Vampiro* strength, Hannah moaned, a thrill shooting through her body at the feel of Zin's cock against her, the feel of his leather vest against her breasts, his leather pants chafing her belly, mound and thighs. She pushed his vest down his shoulders and he released her long enough to let it slide to the floor. Before he could step back to remove his clothing, Hannah's hands were at the fastening of his pants. She undid it and pushed them over his hips. When his cock was released, she slipped her fingers over the long shaft and stroked him from balls to tip and back again as Zin groaned.

She gave him a teasing smile as she looked up at him. "What would you like me to do?"

"Nothing." At her look of surprise he smiled. "It's what I want to do with you. I want to make love to you, Hannah."

Yes, make love. That's what she wanted to do with Zin. Not just fucking, but making love.

He stepped away from her and for that moment she felt an aching emptiness from the loss of contact. In movements just as slow and teasing as her own had been, he kicked off his boots and stripped out of his pants. He smelled so rich, so salty and earthy and so male. Hannah wondered how she had ever lived without the treat of enhanced senses. She never wanted to be human again, if she had to give up this wonderland of sensation.

When he was naked he took her hand and led her to the bed, then gently forced her to lie down with her head resting on one of the satiny pillows. He bent on one knee and brushed a kiss across her knuckles, his gaze remaining focused on hers.

Zin raised his head and said, "Hannah Cordova, will you marry me? Join with me in the oldest of ways?"

She brought her hand to her mouth, tears stinging at the back of her eyes, overcome by the moment. It was so beautiful...her naked warrior on one knee, his black eyes full of love and caring.

The moment she could breathe again, she nodded. "Yes. Most definitely, yes."

His smile warmed her heart even further as he slid into bed and settled himself between her thighs, his arms braced to either side of her. He brought his lips to hers and his long black hair brushed her nipples. She gasped at the sweet sensation and slipped her arms around his neck. For a long time they kissed, and her head began to spin. The kiss became more and more intense, and Hannah was sure she would lose herself in him forever.

And now, forever is a long, long time. Sweet. So, so sweet.

When he finally broke away, she stared up at her handsome warrior, her Eternal Mate and soon to be husband. *Husband.* She was marrying a vampire...and she was a vampire herself.

And she wanted his blood, needed to taste him, to have that most intimate contact. She wanted her essence inside him, and his inside her. She wanted them to feed on each other.

"Yes." He had a pained expression on his face, one of extreme lust and love. "I want to share everything with you. Take my blood as you take me inside you."

Vampiro to Vampiro.

Hannah nodded, unable to speak. Her mouth watered and her fangs protruded from her gums. There was no pain now. No confusion. Only a mind-bending lust to have more of him, and more, and still more.

Zin brought one hand to his cock and placed it at the opening to her channel.

"Now, Zin." Hannah pulled him closer to her, her fingers still locked behind his neck. "I want to experience you in every way imaginable."

With a single thrust, he buried himself deep inside her and held himself still. Hannah cried out with pleasure, and then Zin was offering his neck to her. "Drink deep, *mi amor.*"

The throbbing pulse below his ear called to her. Instinct brought her mouth to his flesh and almost without thought, her incisors had pierced his flesh. She startled at first, but then the warm rush of blood filled her mouth, even as his cock filled her core.

He tasted better than she could have imagined. Like elixir. Like fine, old wine, with no bitterness at all. Her thoughts rushed. She saw past, present and future in one moment. Felt the power of his energy rushing through every inch of her body.

He began to thrust, slow and then harder and harder. Hannah's head spun even more than before as she drank his sweet, sweet blood. She felt his mind within hers, felt the sensations he was experiencing as he pumped in and out of her. Their thoughts were one. Their emotions flowed back and forth, swirling through their veins faster and faster.

Small orgasms rippled through her, her pussy spasming around his cock as she drank from him. Everything whirled around her as his blood slipped over her tongue. Her climax built and built until it nearly shattered her with its intensity. Her fangs retracted and her head fell back against the pillow. More orgasms rippled through her as he continued to drive in and out. He never stopped making love to her as she lapped at the blood trickling from the punctures in his neck and sealed the wound.

"Take my blood," she whispered as her head sank back against the pillow again. "I want to feel it all this time."

He gave a low growl and lowered his face to her neck. He lapped at the soft skin and she shuddered as another mini-orgasm took hold of her. He sank his teeth into her neck as she cried out with pleasure. The silk sheet rubbed against her back with every thrust. She could feel her blood rushing into him, could feel his pleasure, could feel his own climax coming on like a storm.

Another orgasm burst throughout her, an explosion of pleasure that reached to every part of her body. She was hot, so hot. Near to burning. Her fangs extended, and she couldn't help gnashing them over and over. So wild, so feral. Hannah screamed from the depths of her primitive soul.

He raised his head and shouted as he met his own release. Their voices blended in a song unlike any other, a joined note Hannah would never forget. In that instant, she knew they would sing together forever, pushing the limits of music and joy and love, creating a harmony that wouldn't end. *Always. Forever.* The words had so much more meaning now.

Zin continued to thrust his cock in and out of her core until he finally gave a long shuddering sigh. He settled against her, keeping enough weight off her to not crush her, but close enough that she felt the comfort of his heavy body pressed tight to hers. He licked at her neck, sealing the wound, and then moved his blood-warmed lips to hers. They kissed away every drop of life's essence from their lips and then he rolled to his side, taking her with him.

Their bodies were covered in sweat and Hannah smelled the unique blend of their sex and the scent of their blood. She had never been happier in her life.

"I have so much to learn," she murmured. "So much to experience. I haven't even gotten to shape-change yet, but I know I can. I'll be a bird, a white falcon."

"I'll teach you to fly. I'll be with you, beside you, above you, below you." Zin brushed her hair from her face and his dark eyes glittered with emotion. "I'll be everywhere you are, forever and always. I'll sing with you, I'll play my guitar while you serenade the world—and I will never get my fill of you, *mi alma.*"

Hannah felt his words at her center, in the warmth of their mingled blood. She smiled. "We have an eternity for you to prove it, *mi Vampiro.*"

About Cheyenne McCray:

Cheyenne McCray is a thirty-something wild thing at heart, with a passion for sensual romance and a happily-ever-after...but always with a twist. A University of Arizona alumnus, Chey has been writing ever since she can remember, back to her kindergarten days when she penned her first poem. She always knew that one day she would write novels, and with her love of fantasy and romance, combined with her passionate nature, erotic romance is a perfect genre for her. In addition to her adult work, Chey is also published in young adult literary fiction under another name. Chey enjoys spending time with her husband and three sons, traveling, working out at the health club, playing racquetball, and of course writing, writing, writing.

Cheyenne welcomes mail from readers. You can write to her c/o Ellora's Cave Publishing at 1337 Commerice Drive; Suite 13, Stow, Ohio 44224.

Also by Cheyenne McCray:

Erotic Invitation

Seraphine Chronicles 1: Forbidden

Seraphine Chronicles 2: Bewitched

Seraphine Chronicles 3: Spellbound

Seraphine Chronicles 4: Untamed

Wild 1: Wildfire

Wild 2: Wildcat

Wild 3: Wildcard

Wild 4: Wild Borders

Wonderland 1: King of Hearts

Wonderland 2: King of Spades

Wonderland 3: King of Diamonds

Wonderland 4: King of Clubs

Things That Go Bump In the Night 3 – with Mlyn Hurn & Stephanie Burke

About Annie Windsor:

Annie Windsor is 37 years old and lives in Tennessee with her two children and nine pets (as of today's count). Annie's a southern girl, though like most magnolias, she has steel around that soft heart. Does she have a drawl? Of course, though she'll deny it, y'all. She dreams of being a full-time writer, and looks forward to the day she can spend more time on her mountain farm. She loves animals, sunshine, and good fantasy novels. On a perfect day, she writes, reads, spends time with her family, chats with friends, and discovers nothing torn, eaten, or trampled by her beloved puppies or crafty kitties.

Annie welcomes mail from readers. You can write to her c/o Ellora's Cave Publishing at 1337 Commerice Drive; Suite 13, Stow, Ohio 44224.

Also by Annie Windsor:

An Excerpt From
Arda:The Sailmaster's Woman

© Copyright Annie Windsor, 2002.
All Rights Reserved, Ellora's Cave, Inc.

Chapter One

Elise Ashton rubbed her blue eyes and yawned as her cousin Georgia Steel sat down across from her.

The sidewalk café was packed. A dozen yellow plastic tables, two dozen yellow chairs, a brick patio, and a hundred coffee-seeking zombies—it was almost too much for Elise's senses after a sleepless weekend.

She gazed first at Georgia's tired face and then at the sky, wishing she could soar into the low-hanging clouds and escape to Polaris, or maybe Cassiopeia. If only space travel were possible. Surely those star systems had life-sustaining planets, and surely their inhabitants were more interesting than Nashville's natural species: Genus Redneckius.

Then again, if Elise's First Rule held true, the Milky Way wouldn't offer her much better fare than Middle Tennessee.

Elise's First Rule: In the end, all men are boring.

In front of her, gray city streets bustled with typical Monday traffic. Morning heat rose from the pavement in shimmering waves, punctuated by car exhaust and hurrying pedestrians.

"This place looks more like New York every day," Elise muttered. Her long blond hair already lay limp against her shoulders, a testament to July's blistering temperatures.

"Amen." Georgia brushed red bangs behind her ears. The heat didn't seem to be affecting her, but it never did. Georgia was one of those perfect women with a tiny waist, sparkling green eyes, and slender hips. One of those women who worried over losing half a pound, and how many calories were in a carrot stick. If Elise hadn't loved her distant cousin like a sister, she probably would have spiked Georgia's coffee with the highest calorie chocolate syrup *Coffee Stand* had to offer.

A waitress in a white t-shirt with "Latté" scrawled across her plastic-enhanced chest minced over, flashed a phony smile, plopped two cups on their table, and left without so much as a boo or how-do-you-do.

Elise glared after Latté-tits and sighed. "This freaky-dream thing is out of hand. If I don't get some sleep, I'm likely to pour espresso on that woman's head. Perky and rude should be an illegal combination."

"Mm. Well, I think your sexual repression is getting to you." Georgia downed a swig of her morning rations.

"I'm not repressed." Elise shifted in her plastic chair, bringing her knees together and smoothing her black business skirt. It was an unconscious gesture, and Georgia caught it before Elise did.

"Scared something's gonna crawl up in there, girl?"

"No!" Elise let her legs fall open for three seconds, then snapped them back together again. "I mean, not anything I don't want."

Georgia leaned forward, exposing shameless cleavage. "And what does Elise Ashton really, really, gotta-have-it-'til-her-clit-aches want?"

For a few seconds, Elise couldn't speak. Her neck felt warm enough to combust, and she squeezed her coffee mug until her fingers burned. "Oh, please. Let's not start this so early. I'm too sleepy to defend myself."

"You're such a wimp."

"Am not."

"When was the last time you did something wild?"

"I—you—oh, fuck you. Drink your coffee."

Georgia settled back in her seat, bouncing her foot like she usually did after whipping Elise in an argument.

If she hadn't been so sluggish, Elise would have given that bouncing foot a good flick, or at least kicked at one of Georgia's plastic chair legs. Her recent Tai Kwon Do lessons might have made that interesting. As it was, she just smiled at her cousin, filed the exchange for later revenge, and went back to yawning.

"I think it's a trust thing." Georgia grinned. Her foot was still bouncing. "You've been screwed over so many times, you figure why bother, right?"

"Elise's Second Rule: Trust no one but Georgia." Elise sipped at her mocha-almond express, wishing it were magical elixir. "Besides, you've had your own share of screw-overs, m'dear. Face it. Good men, the kind of men who can handle a strong-minded woman—don't exist."

Georgia sighed. "Pessimist. You're probably right, but I'm not willing to give up yet."

Elise took another slug of her espresso, hoping it would keep her eyes open. The State of Tennessee would be grateful if she stayed awake to log in the endless complaints received by the Attorney General's office. No doubt Georgia would be grateful, too, as Elise would be quicker to grab one of the ringing phones. Bossing high-level politicians and lawyers all day kept Elise's mental and emotional claws sharpened, and she could use the workout today.

Georgia and Elise had manned the AG's secretarial staff for almost ten years, since they both finished high school and opted out of college. Georgia didn't go on to higher education because she hated school. Elise didn't go because she couldn't afford it.

She meant to try again once she got older, to study her true passion of astronomy, but there was work. And bills. And Georgia's endless tales of woe from failed relationships. Georgia needed Elise, and Elise needed to be there for her cousin.

Elise's Third Rule: Always take care of Georgia, because she's all you've got.

The two women had grown up together with their only surviving aunt, with little knowledge of their family. As far as Elise was concerned, they hadn't done badly for themselves, either.

At twenty-eight, Elise didn't know if she could even handle the studying involved with going back to school—the grading, the long hours, or even the change from her comfortable, quiet life. She still had her constellation charts and the telescope she bought when she was only twelve. She didn't use it much any more, but every now and then, in the tiny hours of night, when she was almost sure no one could see her, she'd steal a glance at a comet, or watch a meteor shower.

And as the magnificent events unfolded, she would give in to her natural excitement, using her vibrator to bring herself to quick, sharp orgasms as the heavens sparkled.

Now that was something wild.

At least it broke the monotony. But she would never admit it to anyone—especially Georgia. The two women shared an odd instinct, a connection that often let them know more about each other than they should. Elise figured the closeness came from growing up virtually alone, but Georgia always said they were secretly the children of psychic gods.

Whatever.

Elise wasn't spilling about her vibrator or her personal falling stars.

"So, is it still the same dream?" Georgia's lyrical voice cut beneath the crowd noise.

"Yes. Well, no." Elise shifted in her chair, not wanting to lie, but not wanting to mention the nightmares that had recently intruded on her fantasy dreams. In the nightmares, she was a slave, riding in a squalid ship made to look like an inhuman skull. Elise's dreams had a habit of coming true, though not always directly. They were like hints of the future, and the skull-slave scene was definitely not one she wanted to talk about.

"Tell." Georgia leaned forward. Her bright green eyes almost glittered. "I know those dreams are hot."

Elise forced a smile. "Not hot, really. But definitely more intense."

She let the warm coffee run down her throat between sentences. The sensation was almost wicked, especially when paired with thoughts about her nighttime stargazing, and her *good* dreams. The ones about the space pirate with midnight hair and obsidian eyes. Orion himself, with muscles like a god, standing astride the deck of his silver space frigate. Him, she could fuck all night.

"I keep waking up at the wrong times, though." Elise sighed. "Just before the handsome guy makes me come."

"I think you should see your doctor." Georgia glanced at her watch. "Come on. We'll be late."

Elise stood, thinking that if she told her doctor anything about her dreams and fantasies, he'd either take her right there on the exam table or send her to a shrink.

The doc was cute, but he didn't warm Elise's engines. Given that he was rich, smart beyond reason, and very handsome, her lack of response suggested the shrink might be a good idea.

In the end, all men are boring.

However, the thought of being examined with an intimate twist not only made Elise's heart beat faster, but it brought a quick, throbbing ache to the celestial equator between her legs. It had been too long since someone explored her galaxy.

And it was damned hard to find an explorer who knew how to navigate.

If she could find a man, one true, honest man who could excite her every night—a man who would respect her, yet stand up to her—she would wrap her legs tight around that man, fuck him blind, and never let go.

For a few blocks, Elise and Georgia walked in silence as Elise pondered the fact that her standards were so high most men no longer interested her. *In the end...boring.*

Even the good ones. Not that the few relationships she suffered through could be counted as "good ones," but still.

What was she waiting for?

Did she think Orion would drop out of the sky and sweep her away for hot sex on his star boat?

Yeah, right.

Stupid. Exciting, but stupid.

Even if space pirates existed, Elise doubted that any of them would seek wanton sex with her. She just wasn't the type men picked for a wild fucking, no matter how racy her private fantasies became. She was a woman who hooked up with "nice" guys. Clunky, quiet, reserved businessmen who had no clue what to do with a car engine or a clit. Like Bob at work, her supervisor. He'd been making eyes at her for years, and he'd made it clear that if Elise got ready for launch, he was standing by.

Bob was handsome in that former-linebacker sort of way, but jeez. He defined boring, like most men did, in the end, as her first rule so clearly summarized.

Now, Orion—he might be another story.

Enough. Elise forcefully ignored the ache between her legs. *I can't spend my whole day lost in sexual daydreams.*

As her attention returned to reality, she could feel the rush hour crowd jostling by. The air was only getting hotter in the forest of downtown high-rises, and the whole scene made Elise long for a quick trip to the moon.

Instead, she turned left with Georgia, into the alley between two of the tallest government buildings in Nashville. As Georgia cleared the crowd, a man bumped her arm and spilled her coffee all over her blouse.

He didn't even slow down.

Georgia stood stock still for a second, staring after him in disbelief.

Elise noticed the curve of her cousin's perfect breast, nipple hardening beneath the hot liquid. The rich smell of coffee filled her senses, and she wondered what Georgia looked like when she climaxed. Both of her nipples were probably huge then, swollen after so much kneading and sucking.

How would it feel to be fucked by one of the gorgeous male specimens who were never too far from Georgia's beck and call?

Georgia was so free. So reckless.

She probably wore those men out.

Georgia caught Elise's eye, and for one dignity-shattering moment, Elise believed her cousin was reading her mind. She felt her cheeks blaze, hotter than the images still flickering on her mental screen.

A sly grin played on Georgia's elfin features. "Penny for your thoughts."

Elise wished desperately that her face would quit burning. "Not for a million bucks."

What's the matter with me?

"Girl, sometimes, I have the distinct feeling you're wilder than you let on." Georgia grinned again, then sighed and pulled the wet fabric away from her still-saluting nipple. "It's gonna be a hell-Monday. I can tell."

The flames ebbed out of Elise's face. She reached for her bag to get a napkin to help Georgia dry off, then realized there was nothing hanging from her shoulder. "Damn! I must have left my purse at the café. At the counter, when I paid." She stomped her foot. "Damn, damn, damn!"

Georgia looked at her watch. "We don't have time to go back. Five minutes—we'll lose points."

"You head on inside." Elise pointed to the entrance. "I'll run back for it. I can afford a few points to save my license and credit cards."

"Okay, but—hey, I know." Georgia's mischievous smile was unmistakable. "I'll tell Bob you were having female problems. That'll shut him up. He'll probably forget to dock you for being late."

Once more, heat rose to Elise's cheeks at the image of good old Bob thinking about her private bodily functions. "Gee. Thanks. What a true friend."

Georgia giggled, then hurried into the building.

Elise turned and jogged toward the alley entrance. Rush hour was waning. She should be able to get to the café and back in just a few minutes. Bob would have to deal with it. No way was she leaving her wallet—

Smash!

Elise had struck something rock-solid.

She fell hard on her backside, scraping her hands on the dirty alley stones. Pain coursed her spine, and her palms burned.

Legs.

There were legs in front of her, eight to be exact, blocking the alley entrance.

And they looked like leather-clad tree trunks.

The air popped, as if a bubble had dropped around Elise, blocking out the typical city noises and sights. She couldn't see people or cars. There was nothing outside the alley. And nothing in it but her and the tree-trunk legs.

Harsh laughter filled the air.

Elise's heart thundered as she raised her eyes.

Oh, God.

These weren't pirates. At least not the dreamy kind.

The tree-legged men were enormous. Easily seven feet tall, dressed in slick bodysuits and armed with weird silver sticks topped by glowing crescents. And they weren't handsome guys. To a one, they looked like carnival freak shows, human but scale-covered. Long fingernails, spiked teeth—maybe they were part lizard. Or part alligator.

Who could tell?

One thing was for sure, though.

They had skulls tattooed on their scaly necks, and they were green. As in Crayola green.

What are these guys? Actors? Movie monsters?

Elise scrambled to her feet, unable to keep from staring.

The monster closest to her pulsed like a heartbeat, from plain green to neon green and back again. If that was a special effect, it was more advanced than any film crew in Nashville could afford.

But if they aren't actors...

An Excerpt From
SERAPHINE CHRONICLES - FORBIDDEN

© Copyright Cheyenne McCray, 2003.
All Rights Reserved, Ellora's Cave, Inc.

Chapter One

Candlelight flickered across Liana's skin as the last of her clothing pooled at her feet. The scent of jensai blooms floated through the open window on an evening breeze, the balmy air easing over her body like a lover's caress.

Liana stood in the center of her bedchamber and closed her eyes, a vision of the dark stranger filling her senses. As she tilted her head back, her hair brushed her bare buttocks like a whisper of moonlight.

Like she imagined the man's touch would be upon her skin.

Even as she moved her hands to her naked breasts, she was aware of the nordai's passionate night calls outside her cottage. But the raven's cries faded as the stranger's image burned in Liana's thoughts.

Black eyes that had followed her as she had made her way through the tavern. Sensuality simmering beneath the surface of his stare. Ebony hair brushing his broad shoulders. A scruffy hint of a beard along his arrogant jaw. Muscles that flexed with every movement as he towered over her.

Visualizing the stranger's calloused hands upon her body, Liana caressed her taut nipples with her palms. She could almost smell the man's woodsy scent, a hint of which she had caught when she had brushed past him in the tavern. She had shivered from the slight contact, but kept her gaze averted, every nerve ending ablaze with wanting him.

How could she desire a man she had never seen before today?

How could she desire any man when it was *forbidden*?

A moan eased through Liana's lips as the vision of the stranger's touch grew stronger. She imagined his tanned fingers covering her pale breast, his calloused palm chaffing her sensitive nipples. She could feel the black hair on his powerful arms brushing her skin. Her body ached with desire, ached with need. A need she did not understand how to fill.

There was only one being with whom she was supposed to mate—but no. She would not allow that reality to spoil the erotic fantasy weaving through her mind.

She had never mated with a man, for it was forbidden. She had heard lusty tales told by her heart-sister Tierra and the tavern wenches, but Liana had never had such an intense desire to experience such a joining—

Until *him*.

Her belly quivered as she eased one hand down her flat stomach to the tangle of curls between her thighs. Where it was forbidden to touch herself. The place that now ached to be stroked, as though that might ease her wanting of the stranger.

Liana's tresses moved as an extension of her thoughts, sliding over her naked skin like she imagined the stranger might touch her body. His hands would be slow. Gentle. His mouth would feel hot on her lips, her breasts, her belly, leaving a trail of fire wherever he touched.

Burning.

Slipping her fingers between her folds, Liana gasped as she felt the dampness of her desire for the dark stranger. Her other hand continued to knead her nipples as she imagined the man fondling them. Her hair caressed her shoulders down to her hips, and the motion of her fingers grew stronger, more insistent, as she stroked her clit.

But instead of relieving her need for the man, the knot in her belly grew tighter and tighter yet.

She could almost feel the stranger's stubble, rough against her inner thighs. And his tongue—gods, his tongue—laving at her clit that was building with pressure. Building and building and—

A cry of surprise rose in Liana's throat and her eyes flew open as the most exquisite sensations rocked through her. Like a flock of startled blackbirds bursting from their roosts amongst the sacred vines. Like moonlight sparkling across the rainbow sands of Mairi.

Her fingers continued, drawing out the intense feelings until her body could take no more.

Liana dropped to her knees and braced her palms against the rush-covered floor, her hair swinging forward to cover her face. Her breasts swayed and her thighs trembled. Her breath came in short gasps as she struggled to overcome the dizziness that threatened to render her boneless.

When she had strength to move, Liana eased onto her haunches. A sound, ever so slight, pierced the haze still shrouding her confused mind. Through her curtain of hair, she glanced up to see an enormous ebony nordai perched on her windowsill, its black eyes focused intently on her—and a sheath was strapped to its powerful leg. The hilt of a dagger jutted out, a ruby glinting on its hilt like a drop of blood.

Ice chilled Liana's spine. *My gods—what have I done?*

* * * * *

Aric sucked in his breath as the Tanzinite maid collapsed to the floor with the strength of her orgasm. He had known he was breaching Liana's privacy when she had begun to shed her clothing—but he had been too enchanted to move.

And Lord Ir, when she had touched herself, he had nearly come undone. The flushed look of utter surprise and rapture on Liana's face when she had climaxed had been the most beautiful sight he had ever seen.

It had been all he could do to maintain his nordai form. Gods, how he had wanted to fly through her open window, resume his man's body and bury his cock inside her slit, claiming her virgin warmth and fucking her until she screamed her pleasure. How he wanted to be the cause of the ecstasy in those sea green eyes.

Forbidden.

She was of the Tanzinites, the cave-dwellers, and he of the Nordain, the Sky People. Never had the two races mated. Never would they.

Forbidden.

This was the woman who had been named to mate with the Sorcerer Zanden, a Nordain traitor. It was a joining Aric was sworn to prevent—by whatever means deemed necessary.

Forbidden.

The maid sat back upon her haunches, her breasts rising and falling with every breath, her flaxen hair shrouding her delicate features. She was a rare Tanzinite, born without wings, banished from the caves at birth and forced to live on Dair's surface amongst humans and fey folk.

Yet she was perfection. Candlelight danced across her silken skin, as beautiful as a Mairi pearl. Her nipples were the deep rose of the sacred vine's blossoms. The pale curls between her thighs like sea foam. And her hair, moonbeams spilling in shimmering waves past her hips.

His keen senses caught her scent as it rose up to him through the open window. Liana smelled of jensai blooms and moonlight. And of the passion between her thighs, a nectar of which he desired to drink his fill.

A lustful sound escaped Aric—and the maid's attention riveted on him. Even through her fine hair, he saw her sea green eyes widen with shock and fear. For a long moment their gazes remained locked, until Aric forced himself to move.

With a mighty flap of his wings, he took to the dark skies, trying to shove the erotic memories of the Tanzinite woman from his mind. He had a task to complete, and that did *not* include joining with the maid.

Though how in Lord Ir's name he would keep his hands off Liana, he did not know...

Why an electronic book?

We live in the Information Age—an exciting time in the history of human civilization in which technology rules supreme and continues to progress in leaps and bounds every minute of every hour of every day. For a multitude of reasons, more and more avid literary fans are opting to purchase e-books instead of paperbacks. The question to those not yet initiated to the world of electronic reading is simply: *why?*

1. *Price.* An electronic title at Ellora's Cave Publishing runs anywhere from 40-75% less than the cover price of the <u>exact same title</u> in paperback format. Why? Cold mathematics. It is less expensive to publish an e-book than it is to publish a paperback, so the savings are passed along to the consumer.

2. *Space.* Running out of room to house your paperback books? That is one worry you will never have with electronic novels. For a low one-time cost, you can purchase a handheld computer designed specifically for e-reading purposes. Many e-readers are larger than the average handheld, giving you plenty of screen room. Better yet, hundreds of titles can be stored within your new library—a single microchip. (Please note that Ellora's Cave does not endorse any specific brands. You can check our website at www.ellorascave.com for customer recommendations we make available to new consumers.)

3. *Mobility.* Because your new library now consists of only a microchip, your entire cache of books can be taken with you wherever you go.

4. *Personal preferences are accounted for.* Are the words you are currently reading too small? Too large? Too...**ANNOYING**? Paperback books cannot be modified according to personal preferences, but e-books can.

5. *Innovation.* The way you read a book is not the only advancement the Information Age has gifted the literary community with. There is also the factor of what you can read. Ellora's Cave Publishing will be introducing a new line of interactive titles that are available in e-book format only.

6. *Instant gratification.* Is it the middle of the night and all the bookstores are closed? Are you tired of waiting days—sometimes weeks—for online and offline bookstores to ship the novels you bought? Ellora's Cave Publishing sells instantaneous downloads 24 hours a day, 7 days a week, 365 days a year. Our e-book delivery system is 100% automated, meaning your order is filled as soon as you pay for it.

Those are a few of the top reasons why electronic novels are displacing paperbacks for many an avid reader. As always, Ellora's Cave Publishing welcomes your questions and comments. We invite you to email us at service@ellorascave.com or write to us directly at: 1337 Commerce Drive, Suite 13, Stow OH 44224.

Printed in the United States
23302LVS00004B/73-729

9 781419 950285